The Scot's Destiny

HIGHLAND HUNTERS 5

Keira Montclair

DEDICATION

To my grandchildren
You are all an inspiration to me every single day.

CHAPTER ONE

December, 1315 the Highlands of Scotland

MAITLAND MENZIE COULD not fail another female. He forced the bile back down his throat and urged his horse faster.

Dyna Grant's mount galloped wildly ahead of him, bucking and dodging through the trees. "Dyna, I'm directly behind ye. Stay up!" Dyna, Maitland, and Alaric Grant were headed to Grant land. The three had been on patrol for King Robert, but they would be spending the Yule season with their clans. The trip home had been uneventful until Dyna's horse had gone daft.

Something had spooked the beautiful beast, and it ran heedlessly into the forest, tearing through tree branches as if it were a ten-point stag running from arrows.

The risk of failure made his stomach churn, but his conscience drove him forward. Not doing everything possible to help Dyna would only prove him incapable.

And he couldn't fail ever again.

Not the horrific way he'd failed his beloved wife. That harrowing day would never leave him, and haunted him relentlessly every day. Though everyone told him time would heal his wound, it hadn't. Not one wee bit.

"Dyna, lean to the left!" He called as the horse appeared to be leaning right, perilously close to the jagged end of a broken branch.

Dyna Grant was an excellent horsewoman, so she fought, holding her one arm up to protect her face. "He's gone daft! Whoa, Midnight Moon! Whoa!"

She rode a horse descended from her dearest grandsire's famous mount, Midnight. Moon was a massive warhorse, just like all of Midnight's offspring, who were so powerful that they could take on any battle, any creature, any landscape.

Maitland knew this stretch of forest well, so he flew ahead of Dyna when an opening came, urging his horse faster toward a clearing he knew was ahead, a place where he could cut Dyna's horse off, break its flight, then calm it down. Hopefully, it would be enough to stop the beast before Dyna was hurt. As fine a rider as Dyna was, a mad race through a forest was never safe. If she fell at this pace, she'd certainly be injured. The only question was how.

Snap her neck.

Break her leg.

Take out an eye.

Pierce a lung with a sharp branch.

And he'd be partially to blame.

He drove his mount forward, forcing the

thoughts from his mind. He had to continue, do his best, and save Dyna as atonement for failing his wife.

If atonement were possible.

He jerked the reins a bit too forcefully, but his horse responded beautifully, and they crossed the clearing just in time. As they zigzagged in front of Dyna and Midnight Moon, his own horse snorted at the approaching beast. Maitland wasn't sure if it was a warning or a calming note, but it worked.

Midnight Moon slowed, then stopped abruptly; Dyna's momentum jerked her forward, over Midnight Moon's neck, but she hung on and straightened, stroking her horse's neck. Maitland's horse stepped forward and nickered at Midnight Moon, calming the beast even more.

His horse was the hero today, far more than Maitland for certain.

Alaric approached from the other side. "Dyna, what happened?"

"Adder spooked him. The snake slithered in front of him, fortunately kept going or we could have been stopped dead." She dismounted, patting Moon's withers. "Ye are fine, dinnae fear that wee snake." She hugged the horse, then pulled out an apple, and he took it in one bite, crunching it loudly.

"Ye cannae give him one without sharing," Maitland said as his horse thrust his nose forward to look for his own well-deserved treat.

"I know. Good thing yer horse snorted. It caught Moon's attention perfectly. Thank ye,

Maitland. Without yer quick thinking, we might be halfway to the sea by now." She handed Maitland's horse an apple and rubbed his nose.

"I'm glad ye are unhurt, Dyna." Maitland let out a sigh of relief, but it had been his horse who had saved her, not him.

But the ever-wise Dyna gave him a pointed glare as she remounted. "I know that look, Menzie. It was ye who drove the horse and brought it in front of me, not the beast. Ye are the one he listens to. Ye. No one else but ye. Stop torturing yerself."

He nodded, unable to speak. To turn away Dyna's gratitude would dishonor her, but no worthy words would come, catching in his throat and near choking him. Every thought of his wife tore into his soul. Maitland was a haunted man.

Alaric looked overhead and said, "We better keep moving. I dinnae like the feel in the air nor the look of the sky." Highland winters could be brutal, and no one knew it better than they did.

"Aye, I'd like to be in front of a warm fire before those clouds open on us. We should be there within the hour," Dyna agreed, keeping her horse behind Maitland's just to keep it anchored. "We canno' afford another snowstorm like we had near Inverness."

They moved forward silently, moving the horses at a brisk but safe pace with the aim of hitting Grant land soon, and making it to the castle gates not long after. It wasn't the time to talk, which of course left Maitland alone with his memories.

Maitland had been haunted ever since the day

his wife had died at only two and twenty winters. A lovely lass ten years his junior but his match in every other way. It had been more than five years now, and the grief and anger of that day had never faded. They'd both been captured by the English, held in the dungeon of some Scottish castle he couldn't remember, together at first, but then they'd been separated.

He'd listened to her screams for hours until they'd faded into whimpers and then finally gone silent altogether.

He'd pulled so hard against the chain that bound him to the wall, he'd thought they might rip free. If he'd had a blade, he'd have cut his own hand off so he could go to her aid, but he'd been able to do nothing. They dragged her dead body into his cell, and he'd held her and sobbed for hours.

He'd been so haunted that they could get no more information from him. He'd been devastated enough that he couldn't even recall any questions they asked him. No matter what they threatened him with, it didn't matter. Nothing mattered once he'd lost his dear wife. His sweet Nesta had been beaten to death. Or so he'd guessed. Her face had only sported one bruise, and he chose not to look at the rest of her body out of respect. She'd been wrapped in a heavy blanket and he'd left it. She'd always been cold while she carried their bairn. How he'd loved stroking her rounded belly as they lay together in bed. How he'd longed to meet his first child, whose time to enter the world was almost upon them.

Both Nesta and their unborn bairn had died alone in a cold castle, and he'd been unable to help them.

How could he ever live with himself?

As time passed, he'd learned to put the pain aside when he had something else to accomplish, but every once in a while, when his memories overpowered his senses, he made a trip up north to Clan Grant. His friends here helped him ease the pain, helped him understand that it was not entirely his fault.

"Alaric, how close are we? I haven't been minding the landmarks." Alaric was the son of Jamie Grant, who, along with Jamie's brother Connor, led the clan as chieftain.

"We just crossed onto Grant land, so not far now. One of my uncles or my sire will be here soon enough—their patrols are frequent. Who do ye wish to visit with? Ye said ye were hoping to stay for a few days and spend time with friends."

"Connor and Finlay. The three of us enjoy talking about the old days when Alex was still alive."

Dyna pointed to the view of Grant Castle up on the hill. "We are nearly there. My sire will be pleased to see ye, Maitland. He always enjoys yer conversations." The castle had grown over the years, with six towers now and three stories to its keep. Each of Alex and Maddie Grant's children had their own tower for their family, though Maeve, the only one yet unwed, lived in the main keep. Jake, the eldest, had passed away several years ago, and now his son Alasdair and his family occupied that tower.

"And ye must be eager to hug yer wee ones," Maitland said to Dyna. "How many now?"

"Three. Two lasses and one lad. He's the youngest, but he loves to fight with his sisters. I hope Derric dinnae lose his mind. I brought him a new sword from Uncle Gregor, and I have new bows for the lasses from Aunt Merewen. And leggings too."

Maitland couldn't help but smile thinking about Dyna's girls and their bows. They were both petite but powerful, acting like wee archers, just like their mother. How he wished he and Nesta had been able to raise a family. He'd often thought on the one child they'd lost. Had it been a wee laddie or a lassie? Perhaps having a bairn to dote on, to keep his mind busy, to be a bit of Nesta still in his life, would have eased the pain. It was the only reason he still went on patrols, to keep himself busy and to help others.

He didn't want anyone to go through what he had.

But every once in a while he had to return to Clan Grant. Connor Grant and Finlay MacNicol knew how to help him, because they had both been through something similar. Connor's wife had been tortured with spiders by a man who seemed to delight in causing fear, and Finlay's wife Kyla had been in a similar situation to Maitland and Nesta. Finlay had finally gotten her out, but he often spoke about how hard it had been when her father came to claim her. They hadn't been married at the time, so Finlay feared Alex Grant would put a sword through his belly when he found them together. But the man had been grateful when he'd seen Finlay's involvement had been rescuing her, not causing her injury. Even Jamie helped him deal with his loss. He'd nearly lost Gracie in marriage to another, and he'd often said he wouldn't have been able to tolerate even so much as that.

Talking with any of them helped him get through his darkest moments. He tried his best not to allow his parents to see his grief anymore. They'd seen enough.

Alaric shouted over his shoulder. "I see a chieftain or two headed this way." He grinned and let out the Grant war whoop, which was answered with five others.

Maitland had to smile. He loved this clan nearly as much as his own and Clan Ramsay. The clans had maintained their close ties for decades now.

Connor and Jamie Grant, co-lairds of the clan, came around the bend with wide smiles and welcoming hoots. "Dyna, yer husband is sorely glad ye are home. And yer lasses cannae wait to see ye."

"And Sandor?" Derric and Dyna's only son was fondly named after Alexander Grant, and his unusual name came about because Alick, Elshander, and Alasdair were already chosen by others in the clan.

"Sandor is well. When we left, he was busy watching yer daughters totally confuse Derric."

Dyna shook her head, her nearly white hair

bouncing in the wind, even though it was tied neatly back at her crown. "Grandmama didnae help?"

"They had Sela totally confused too." Her father grinned. "Sure was fun watching the two connive against their father."

Jamie Grant interrupted. "Enough of yer family. Alaric, ye are hale?

"Aye, Da. All is well on Cameron land, as Uncle Connor has probably told ye. We havenae seen much trouble this time. Seems to be a wee bit quieter at present."

Maitland loved listening to the banter, but a cold breeze whipped up out of nowhere, bringing his attention to their surroundings. Sure enough, a swirl of gray clouds appeared overhead, moving quickly across the sky and bringing the threat of poor weather closer by the moment. Darkness descended quickly, the last of the sun dimming behind the storming clouds.

"Snowstorm or rain coming? The temperature is close enough to be either one." Maitland lifted his head to the wind. "Glad we are nearly there. I have a fear of getting stuck in the middle of the Highlands in a blizzard. We just met one in Inverness not long ago. One is enough!"

"'Tis only one way to handle that," Jamie said. "Find the nearest cave. It can kill ye if ye try to find yer way out of a blizzard. The snow has a way of mesmerizing ye and sending ye in the wrong direction."

Dyna shifted in her saddle. "Let's move faster. There is a current of warmer air that I dinnae like. Warm fights against the cold, and 'tis never a good battle." She tugged her scarf tighter around her neck and sent her horse into a gallop. Maitland followed. He trusted Dyna's instincts over his own, even when they didn't agree.

They were nearly there when the clouds opened up, drenching them in a cold rain that chilled his bones in a way he'd not felt in a long time.

"Go, Dyna." She was ahead of him and slowed because her horse fussed in the rain. Connor came along beside her and grabbed Midnight Moon's reins.

"We're almost to the stables. We'll get them all inside the main building. It's large enough to hold them all." Clan Grant had so many horses that they had multiple stables around the castle. Connor whistled sharply as they approached, and Maitland was glad to see a pair of lads opening the doors on the end to allow them all inside.

Maitland shivered as he dismounted and led his horse inside. The beasts were reacting to the change in the weather, acting up enough to make him fear they'd bolt.

"Here now," he said to his horse, rubbing his withers and leading him to a stall where he could brush him down and give him some oats. Once he had the animal calm, he went back out to help the others, but he caught something out of the corner of his eye through the door, which had been left ajar.

Someone raced across the landscape carrying a basket, heading toward the keep from the nearby orchard. He wouldn't have paid much attention because the woman could easily get inside the keep, but then she lost her balance in the sheeting rain and fell flat on her back into a pile of stones.

She didn't move, not even making an effort to get up. Maitland had no thought but to help. He hurried out, reached her, and bent down to help her up, but the lass had been knocked unconscious.

He lifted her into his arms, not the easiest thing to do in the rain. The wool of her skirt was sodden, and she had a substantial figure— just the type he liked, if he didn't have to carry a lass. Her head fell back, her hood dangling freely. Rain pelted her face, but she showed no reaction. Maitland stared at her, surprised that she could look beautiful even drenched and in the middle of a storm.

Connor came up behind him. "Is that Maeve? Get her inside. I'll get the door so ye can get her into the keep. She'll have a goose egg from that knock, to be sure."

The sky lit up with lightning as they hurried through the courtyard toward the keep. Jamie and Dyna rushed up behind them. "What happened?"

"She took a fall and hit her head," Maitland said, doing his best to protect her face from the pelting rain.

Once inside, Connor led him to the healing chamber off the hall, once used as Alex and Maddie's chamber. "Set her on the bed. We'll go find Gracie."

The others left, and he set Maeve down and

hung his mantle on a nearby peg. Its drips made quiet splatting sounds on the stone floor. But he wasn't as drenched as poor Maeve was. He sat her up and did his best to remove her own mantle, though it was a struggle because her coat was so heavy with water and she still hadn't woken. But as he tugged on one sleeve of the garment, her eyes fluttered open and she caught sight of him.

"Where am I? What happened?"

He got her coat off and hung it by the fireplace. He returned to sit on the edge of the bed, and she leaned against him. He was glad to offer whatever support he could. Then she pulled back and stared at him.

"Am I dead?"

"Nay, Maeve. Ye are in the healing chamber. Ye hit yer head."

She paused, looking around her as an eerie golden glow appeared around her head. He couldn't drag his eyes away, though he leaned back to see the whole of her. "Maeve?"

There was no mistaking what he saw. She looked exactly like an angel.

An angel from Heaven.

CHAPTER TWO

MAEVE'S HEAD POUNDED as though someone had hit it with a hammer, the pain nearly unbearable. And she was covered in mud from head to toe. She sat up on the bed, her hand gingerly going to the back of her head. She winced as her fingers brushed the bump she found there.

Gracie rushed in, her two daughters behind her, but she stopped to speak with Maitland. "How did ye find her?"

"I saw her slip out of the corner of my eye. She'd just passed the stack of stone ye keep for repairing the wall. And it knocked her out. She just came to a moment ago. I tried to get her wet clothes off, but only what was appropriate."

"Many thanks to ye, Maitland. We're blessed ye were here to see it. My daughter will find ye a chamber where ye can don some dry clothing and then find some food to warm ye."

Maitland turned about to look at Maeve one more time, so she whispered, "My thanks to ye, Maitland." A blush heated her skin like a warmed blanket, and she wished to stop it but knew it was nearly impossible. She'd always blushed too easily.

"'Twas my honor to help ye, Maeve," he said, his gaze locking on hers enough to send that blush inside and deep into her belly. "I wish ye a quick healing."

Maitland was a very handsome man even when he was drenched, his dark hair in wet waves, giving him a mysterious look. He set his jaw before he turned around, and she couldn't help but wonder what he was thinking. He had eyes the color of the darkest wood on the trees and skin a dark bronze from the sun. She didn't mind the dark scruff across his jaw, making her think he kept his chin clean shaven unless he was traveling.

Or perhaps he was like some men who grew a beard as the weather turned colder. Winter was upon them, and as her dear father used to say, "'Twill warm my face, Maeve. Dinnae fear my beard."

She let out a deep sigh, wishing her father were still here. Maitland left and Gracie approached, her hand going to the bump on the back of Maeve's head. "'Twill ache for a while, my dear. We should get ye out of those wet clothes first, then I'll find ye a potion to help ye with the pain. And a cold compress will help the swelling go down."

"I would like to get out of these clothes," she said, a small shiver coursing through her.

"What happened?" Gracie asked as she tugged on her gown to remove it.

"I was trying to save the last of the pears and

apples from the orchard when the storm hit. I only had a few moments to run inside, and I lingered too long. I do not know where my basket landed, but the few pears are probably mush by now. The trees did not bear fruit the way they usually do. I dinnae know why."

"We have plenty of food, and ye know that. It was a dry summer so the harvest was a little low, but no' enough to affect us. Ye needn't worry, Maeve. Every orchard has good years and scant years." Gracie pushed the stray hairs that had escaped her plait behind her ears. Up close, Maeve noticed quite a few white hairs mixed in with the gold, but they were not noticeable from afar.

Did Maeve's blonde hair have white through it? At six and thirty, she was no longer a lassie. Her father had been correct when he'd told her that her time to find a husband was running out.

It was probably long gone already.

Maeve had no idea who her true parents were, but she had adored her adoptive parents, Alex and Maddie. Her heart had broken when she lost each of them, grieving no less than her adoptive siblings. And she took it as part of her duty to contribute to the clan—she was a Grant as loyal and true as any other. Her greatest contribution was the orchard she and Maddie had planted many years ago. They'd made a small area inside the curtain wall so all the fruit would be for the clan.

Her father had planted an orchard outside the wall, but she'd only tended it when Alex had been here to protect her. Since his death, she'd been too frightened to go outside the wall. She might have to find someone to go with her so she could make sure they had plentiful stores before winter truly set in. She knew who she wanted to ask.

"Why is Maitland here?" she asked.

"I think he came with Dyna. He likes to visit with Connor, Jamie, and Finlay." Once Gracie finished helping Maeve clean up and get into a dry gown, she moved to the center table to mix a potion. "Does anything else hurt ye, Maeve?"

"Just my pride. Many thanks for your help— getting clean helped as much as anything could. But how did I get here? I don't recall anything except slipping in the mud."

"Maitland found ye and carried ye in."

She gasped. "But I'm too heavy. He did? Truly?"

"Aye. Maeve, ye arenae that heavy. Ye are built strong, and so is Maitland. Ye are fine. Dinnae think on it any longer." Gracie winked at her. "Aye, and Maitland is fine, as well. Do ye not think so?"

She did think so. Indeed, her mind couldn't stray to anything else but Maitland Menzie.

How she wished he was interested in her. She'd often thought of him because he was the same age as she was. Nearly forty winters they were, and he was one of the few men her age who wasn't married. She'd dreamed of marrying and having bairns of her own when she was younger, but she would have to let that wish go. She was too old now. And though her father had forever been pushing her to marry, she'd never had the nerve to mention anyone's name to him, especially someone from another clan.

Her heart had sunk a little when Maitland had married Nesta, but she'd been glad to see him happy and sorry for his grief when she died. She knew the loss of his wife lingered and kept him from seeking out another. But that sorrow meant that he loved deeply and would be fiercely loyal to any who earned his esteem.

If only time had healed his heart.

Gracie handed her the goblet filled with the potion, then said, "Ye should speak to Maitland again. I think the two of ye would be a good match, Maeve. Ye know Papa wished for ye to marry. Why no' Maitland?"

Maeve promptly dropped the goblet, spilling it everywhere.

Gracie's eyes twinkled with mirth. "I know what that means, Maeve!"

Maitland sat down on the bed in the chamber they often gave him and thought on what he'd seen. Maeve had indeed had a golden aura around her head. What the hell did that mean? And why hadn't it happened when someone else could be a witness to the strange occurrence?

He shook his head, wondering if he'd fallen asleep for a moment and dreamed the odd vision. No one would believe him if he mentioned it. He was exhausted after their long journey, as everyone would no doubt point out to him.

There. That was all there was to it. Now that

he'd settled that in his mind, he searched the chest of drawers for a clean tunic. The Grants always kept spare clothing in their guest chambers. He forced his mind away from how drawn he'd felt to Maeve. He'd merely been without a woman for too long. Maeve was not for him, and it was improper to think on her too much. He owed his devotion to his wife, Nesta. She was the only one for him.

Or was she? He wondered what she would say if her ghost were here to ask. Would she be upset if he found another after five years? Or would she wish for him to find a companion?

He changed his clothes, used a cloth to dry his long hair, then washed his face and hands before heading back downstairs to the great hall. There, Connor stood near the sideboard, filling two goblets with ale just as a serving lass brought out two meat pies.

"Perfect," Maitland said as he approached Connor, who held one of the goblets out to him. "My thanks to ye. I'll warm myself by the fire for a moment before I enjoy the meat pie."

Connor moved to a chair by the fire, and Maitland followed. "I owe ye a debt of gratitude for calming Dyna's horse. She told me what happened. We dinnae see many adders around here, especially in this weather, but the horses dinnae like them one bit."

"She would have been fine. Ye know yer daughter can handle any horse." Maitland took a chair and stared at the fire. What would he do if anything happened to Dyna, who he loved like his own blood? Sometimes the responsibility of the patrol became too much for him, thus his trip to Grant land for camaraderie and conversation.

"Ye came when we were no' expecting ye. What is in yer head now?" Connor asked, leaning back in his sire's huge chair.

The man could always guess what Maitland was thinking, as if they were born as twin brothers. "The usual. The trip to Inverness when Ceit and Brin had to spend a night in the cave. Ysenda broke her leg. Lewis is hurting too. I wonder if I could have prevented any of it. I cannae but think I let them down."

"Ye went back for them and they were there, aye?"

"Aye." He sighed. "'Tis a good thing. Marcas nearly forced their marriage when we returned to Black Isle, and it was before they were ready, but he calmed down. Brin was no' willing to propose at Marcas's order. He wanted it on his terms."

"And if I know Logan Ramsay's granddaughter, she was no' anxious to be forced into marriage either."

Maitland snorted, then whispered, "They are all alike, are they no'?"

Connor stared at him, a wide grin on his face. "Are they?"

"Aye. Isla, Reyna, Ceit, Ysenda, Thea. All stubborn, strong women and such powerful archers, much like yer daughter. Their skill with the bow is astounding, and I couldnae tell ye who is the best. Gwyneth is so proud of all of them."

"As is Logan, I am sure."

"But he'll no' admit it." They chuckled over that, knowing the truth of it.

"Of course no'," Connor said. "While in our clan, it was the lads who were alike. Alasdair, Alick, and Els, warriors all. Dyna was the only lass in the group."

"But she's one of the strongest, man or woman."

"Aye, she is. Sela and I are so proud of her, as we are of Astra and Hagen. We've been truly blessed."

"And how was Grandmama with the bairns while their mama was away?" Maitland knew Dyna loved to jest about how the lassies could confuse their grandmother. Sandor basically did as he wished, ignoring the two lasses, and that drove his sisters to distraction.

"Ye'll see. They'll be about on the morrow once they learn ye are here."

Maitland grabbed his meat pie and took a bite, chewing slowly as he stared at the flames. How he wished he was married and had bairns of his own. He didn't understand why fate had sent him down a different path.

"What news of Maeve? Does Gracie think all will be fine with her?" Connor asked.

"Aye. She took a hard fall. That bump of hers will pain her for a while. Why was she outside in this weather? Everyone knows it's wise to keep an eye on the sky, especially at this time of year." Maitland brushed the crumbs from his fingers after savoring the last bite of his pie. "Delicious."

Connor frowned. "Maeve has struggled ever

since we lost Da. I probably shouldn't tell ye this, but I trust ye'll keep it to yerself. She wakes many nights due to nightmares. Always has, which is why she slept in a bed in my parents' chamber when she was young. She and Papa had a strong bond—she never had much interest in any lads about, preferring to stay close to Da. No one knows what her first few years were like, but they were no' good. She doesn't remember anything from her nightmares, just darkness, but the fear willnae leave her."

"So now that Alex is gone, does she no' wish to find a husband to protect her? Someone hurt her when she was a bairn, is my guess, and that's who she fears. Someone evil from her past."

"I would agree with ye, but 'tis too soon. Every Grant would guard her if she asked. For now, she stays within the castle wall, spending all her time fussing over the orchard."

"But yer largest orchard is outside the wall." Would not the larger orchard need more attention than the smaller? Apparently Maeve approached things differently, though her actions confused him.

"Aye, and Da planted many of those trees, but she's too afraid to go that far on her own. She used to tend those trees with Papa, but without him, she will not venture that far. Maeve and Mama planted the inner orchard many years ago, and it's as if each orchard represents Mama and Papa. They must grow and flourish or Maeve frets as if Mama or Papa themselves were feeling poorly. This summer was a wee bit dry, and the harvest suffered from it. Not enough to worry us, but it surely worries Maeve."

"'Tis a sad situation. Mayhap she will grow more confident with time. Or is it because we are nearing the anniversary of Alex's death?"

"That could be. But tell me—have ye still no' found someone yerself? I was hoping with all the lasses ye are around on patrol that ye would surely find one who suited ye."

Maitland shook his head. "They are too young, Connor. Lovely lasses, but too young for me. All I try to do is keep them alive. They are all young enough to think themselves invincible. Ye know what that age is like. Besides, I'm related to many of them."

"Then find an older woman. Our way of life has left more than one widowed too young, as ye are. There must be a few on yer land. Or on Cameron land."

"I hope I'm ready to do so soon."

"After five years, ye should be ready. Think on it. Anyone. There are many women who have hoped ye'd consider them, as ye know."

Maitland scowled. "Not yet."

Probably never.

CHAPTER THREE

M AEVE STOOD BY the gate, her sister Kyla
next to her.

"I'll hold yer hand if ye like, Maeve. Ye need to get past this fear," Kyla said.

Maeve fought the tears threatening to wet her cheeks. "I wish to go, I truly do, but my feet will not move. But perhaps I can go with you." She paused to take a deep breath and convince herself that this was the right time to move forward. It was indeed. "It is time for me to face my fears. Your support helps me be strong, Kyla." She adored her dearest sister, especially because she never faulted her for talking like their mother. Maddie's mother had been English, and she'd never picked up the Scots burr. Maeve had come to the Grants with the same English accent as Maddie, though she had no memory of whether either parent was English or Scottish. Kyla spoke like a Scot.

A deep voice interrupted them. "Maeve, how do ye fare this morn?" Maitland approached them and Kyla waved him over. A little too happily, in

Maeve's opinion, but since she liked Maitland, she wouldn't argue.

"I am well, Maitland. Again I must thank you for bringing me into the keep yestereve." She didn't bring her gaze up to his because she knew her eyes would give her true feelings away. The man was just too handsome.

"Where are ye headed?" He stood next to her, his large frame blocking the bit of sun peeking out between the gray clouds.

"I came out to find my basket I dropped, hoping to salvage some of yesterday's harvest, but the fruit didn't survive the storm. That had been the last of it from the inner orchard, so Kyla and I were thinking of checking the larger orchard." She looked to her sister and smiled. "Unless you've changed your mind."

"Och, nay, sister," Kyla exclaimed. "We have someone to protect us just as Da always did, so 'tis a good day to go. Do ye no' agree?"

"I do agree. Maitland, are you agreeable? Da always came with me before, and I feel his absence deeply in the orchard. But if you will come, perhaps it will help." And he would help her get over her fear. She was too old to have these ridiculous worries of something bad happening just because Alex Grant was not here to protect her. There were many strong men and women in Clan Grant, and they would all come to her aid if something happened. She knew that truth without a doubt, yet her belly still turned upside down as soon as she headed toward the orchard.

"'Twould be a great pleasure to join ye, Maeve," Maitland said. "Are ye ready?"

Maitland stood there looking gorgeous and awaiting her response. It was time to push herself. And she did wish to collect whatever fruit she could before it all turned to mush. This was her duty for her clan. Her father had helped her choose her work long ago, asking her if she liked apples and pears. Now she looked back on his cunning ways with a smile. He knew she loved autumn fruit, but he didn't tell her minding the orchards would be her job. It was his way to let her choose it. After explaining that everyone in the clan was expected to make a contribution to help others, she'd chosen apple-picking, and he'd helped her ever since. The pears were just an added blessing, their sweet flesh one of her great delights, but they weren't around as long as the apples.

"I'm ready." She took a step forward, and they all moved toward the orchard. Ignoring the tremors that began inside her, she vowed not to turn back this time. Maitland had his sword with him, and he would protect her, no matter who might come.

Maitland led the way, his gaze scanning the area. "I think ye still have apples to pick on some trees, Maeve. 'Tis a mighty large orchard. Ye planted this?"

"Papa did when I was much younger, but I helped." She was proud of her part in it. The orchard bore so much fruit each autumn, more than they could eat some years. It had been such a delight to see how the trees grew each year, sometimes causing her to giggle when they came out for their first visit each spring. This year's harvest had been a little thin, but it was enough. There were already barrels in the cold cellar full of fruit.

She made it to the edge of the orchard, which tucked up against the forest on two sides. The forest caused the worst of her fears. It was dark beneath the trees, and that darkness filled her nightmares. Maeve could never remember what made her scream loud enough to wake herself and the family, but darkness was always there.

Her parents had her speak to different people about her dreams—them first of all, but also wise women and clergy and others who'd experienced similar terrors and overcome them, but she never remembered anything more than the darkness and the feeling of something creeping up her arms, the back of her neck, the…

Oh, but she had to pay attention to the present.

Maitland moved over to one tree and plucked several ripe apples, dropping them into Kyla's outstretched plaid. Fortunately, they hadn't experienced a heavy snowfall yet, or the fruit would all be on the ground. Yesterday's storm had knocked some of the fruit to the ground, but much still clung to the branches, thanks to the screening forest trees.

Maeve took a deep breath and began to gather the windfalls from the ground, sorting the ones good enough to keep from those too bruised or soft. The horses would enjoy the overripe ones, but they would ruin the winter stores, so they had to be kept separate.

She froze after only a few steps at the sound of horse's hooves. She spun in a circle, looking for the source, but saw nothing.

"Maeve, what's wrong?" Kyla asked.

"Maeve, who are ye looking for?" Maitland called out.

"The horses." She whirled around again, the sounds getting louder.

Kyla cocked her head and listened. "I dinnae hear any horses."

Maitland approached her, and she reached for him just as the group of five horses broke through the forest and headed straight for her. She screamed, clutching Maitland's mantle, praying he could save her.

"Maeve! What is it?" Kyla hurried closer, looking frantically around.

"The men. Do not let them get me. Please!"

"What men?"

Maitland tucked her close to his side. "I'll no' let them take ye, Maeve."

She leaned against him, collapsing into his arms, sobbing. Kyla lay a hand on her shoulder and spoke soothing words to her while Maitland stroked her back.

"'Tis no one there, Maeve. 'Tis yer imagination. But look at them with yer mind's eye and tell me who they are." Maitland held her and whispered in her ear.

She opened her eyes, and her gaze scanned the area again, but he was right. No one was there.

Maeve's jaw clenched as something changed inside her. This time, she was angry. Here she was with a man she was attracted to, and he'd witnessed her secret fear bursting out of her. Why now? Usually her nightmares were just that—nighttime terrors. Why would they suddenly pop into her mind in front of Maitland? How dare they ruin her first day in this beloved orchard since Alex's death?

Maeve stared up at Maitland and gave him her honest answer. "I cannot see their faces, Maitland. But I thank you for being here with me. You protected me from them, though not with your sword."

How she prayed he wouldn't hate her for her foolishness.

Maitland nearly scooped her up in his arms and carried her inside again, but Kyla stayed his hand. "Nay. Allow her to face this fear. Whatever it is, she must discover what is driving it."

Maeve's gaze scanned the area again, but her face showed how defeated she felt.

Kyla pushed her a bit more. "Are ye sure ye can see nothing about them, Maeve? There must be some clue for ye. A color of plaid, the number of horses, something to tell ye what clan they are from. Or are they English?"

She let out a deep sigh of frustration. "All I see is five riders. I know they are men, but no more. I canno' see them. Forgive me."

"Does this happen often?" Maitland had never

heard such a heart-wrenching sound as Maeve's scream. Nesta's screams had been different somehow—screams of struggle and pain. Maeve's had been pure terror.

But terror of what? Why?

"Nay. I've never experienced anything like that—visions of things that were not there—while awake."

Jamie and two guards came running toward them. "What happened? Need ye assistance?"

Kyla waved them back and shook her head behind Maeve's back, which made Maitland wonder exactly what was happening. Was she being honest on this being the first time it happened?

Maeve, too, waved a hand at Jamie in dismissal. "I don't know what happened, but I am fine. No reason to concern yourself at all, Jamie. We'll go back to picking apples."

"Good to hear it," Jamie said. "Since I'm out here, Kyla, I'll pass on that Chrissa is looking for ye."

"I'll go see what she wishes. Maeve, ye'll stay with Maitland?"

She peered up at him and said, "If Maitland does not mind, I'd prefer to stay. I see nearly a barrel of apples that we could pick. Snow will be here soon and there is no time to waste."

"I put two baskets behind those trees the other day. Use those." Jamie pointed to a corner of the orchard they hadn't reached yet.

Maitland squeezed Maeve's hand before stepping away to retrieve one of Jamie's baskets.

He was glad she was willing to stay and glad that she trusted him. He wished to get to know her better.

"I'll hold it so ye can fill it."

"Perfect," she exclaimed with a wide smile on her face.

She was as beautiful as any woman he'd ever seen, and when she smiled, something inside him lit up. Her hair was the color of straw and her eyes the same blue as the flowers in the summer fields. The cold made her cheeks as rosy as could be, and he yearned to plant a kiss on one. Would she allow it? Would he?

Aye, he would. Something had happened to his heart—perhaps it was his vision of Maeve as an angel. Perhaps holding her in his arms and wishing for nothing so much as offering her safety and security. He would always love Nesta, but he knew in his heart she wouldnae want him to grieve forever. Their happiness had been that of youth. Now, with so much life behind him— he and Maeve might understand each other's needs in a deeper way.

Maeve was no young maiden. She had her own sorrows, it was clear. And her own experiences. He needn't hesitate to show her how he felt. She should be aware of the ways of men and women. Even though she wasn't married, that didn't mean there hadn't been a man in her life at one time or another.

Maeve moved over to the edge of the orchard where there appeared to be a large number of apples still on the trees. "Here, Maitland. There are so many beautiful ones right here."

He brought the basket over and reached for the ripe fruit. Maeve harvested from the lower branches while he plucked the apples far above her head. "They'll be wasted if we dinnae grab them now. Snow is nearly upon us."

"And those green ones too. They will be wonderful in fruit tarts." She glanced over at the man who'd held her during her worst fear. "Will you return home for Yule?" she asked.

"Probably. I hope we dinnae need to do much patrolling in the coldest months of winter. And I'm anxious to see my brothers and my parents. Tad's wife is about to have their third bairn, and I'd like to see the wee one."

"I'll wager you are good with the children, Maitland."

"Aye," he said, trying not to sound like he was bragging. But he was great with the bairns. Tad called him a big bear that the youngsters clung to, and it was true. "Tad has two laddies, and they like to hang all over me, but mostly because I have fun tossing them about and swinging them."

"I can picture you doing what my father used to do. He would hold his arms out whenever we were in the loch, and his three grandsons would swing on him as if they were climbing a tree."

That image made him laugh. "I do recall Alex doing that. Alasdair, Els, and Alick were relentless." He loved bairns—lads and lasses. He'd thought once he'd have at least six or seven of his own. But it wasn't to be.

He pulled down two more apples with one big hand when something else fell out of the tree. A feather.

"Oh, I want that feather. It is a beauty. The wee ones will love it." Maeve placed the apples into the basket and chased the feather, but she couldn't quite reach it. She broke into a fit of giggles every time she missed it and the draft from her swinging arm sent it back above her head.

Maitland chased after the feather himself, looking like a fool, he guessed, but he didn't care. His leaps and her small jumps made them both laugh until they made the mistake of jumping at the same time. They bumped into each other midair.

They landed together with a huff on a pile of leaves, each flat on their back. He turned to look at her and was instantly lost in her blue eyes. He rolled and perched above her on one elbow, taking in her sweet scent and the creaminess of her skin. It was as if the world stopped around them.

"Maeve, would it upset ye if I gave ye a kiss?"

She said nothing but shook her head, her gaze locked on his. He kissed her, softly at first, tasting her lusciousness, the sweetness of the apple she'd been enjoying still on her lips. His hand came up to cup her cheek, and he rubbed the pad of his thumb across her soft skin. She parted her lips, and he groaned, accepting what she offered, angling his mouth to delve deeper. He hadn't expected her to be so willing. He'd expected her to be more timid.

But she was not timid at all. He stroked her tongue with his own, and she let out the smallest of whimpers, the kind that went straight to his member. He ended the kiss then and there to keep from going too far, then rose to his knees and held his hands out to her, helping her up. They got to their feet hand in hand.

"Ye give the sweetest of kisses, Maeve," he said, longing for another but resisting the urge. He had to ask. "Ye've never been betrothed to anyone?"

"Nay," she said, chewing on her lower lip before blurting out, "Maitland, I'm not a maiden. Someone stole my maidenhead long ago."

Her honesty surprised him—it seemed an odd time for the confession—but it told him how nervous she was. "Maeve, that matters no' to me."

"And I can never marry, because I'll never leave Grant Castle."

He narrowed his gaze, thinking on where he'd heard something similar. Ceit. Ceit had sworn to never leave Ramsay land because it was the only place she could be a female archer and not be ridiculed because of it. Or so she'd believed. She'd changed her mind once she'd fallen in love with Brin Cameron. But he wondered why Maeve had decided never to leave Grant Castle. Though the earlier episode, with her phantom riders, gave him an idea of the reason.

"Maeve, 'twas just a kiss." He caught how she wilted at the comment, and he recalled how different men and women were. What mattered to him was how she acted in his arms, but what mattered to her was what he said. Nesta had taught him that. He decided to cushion his comment. "I liked our kiss verra much and I hope ye'll grant me another, but it was nae marriage proposal."

"Oh!" She blushed.

He grinned and then winked at her. "I'd like to get to know ye, Maeve."

"Forgive me for being so rash."

"Ye are no' rash, but tell me why ye feel that way. I know someone else who felt the same."

"Because this is my home. I've only lived here. And…" Then she shook her head. "Never mind."

He wondered what she was not saying. If they were meant to be, she'd tell him when she was ready.

"I hope ye'll feel comfortable telling me someday, but ye dinnae have to say aught now. One kiss dinnae entitle me to all yer thoughts." He reached for her hand and squeezed it.

Her answer couldn't have surprised him more.

"I've never been off Grant land since my fifth summer. And I do not recall anything before that. I feel safer here." Her gaze dropped to the ground, he guessed out of embarrassment. He did not know anyone who'd never left their clan lands for any reason. "Anything might happen, out there. It is easier to stay here."

Maeve Grant had more to her than met the eye.

CHAPTER FOUR

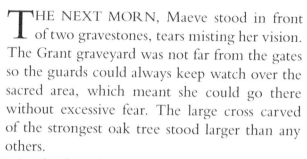

THE NEXT MORN, Maeve stood in front of two gravestones, tears misting her vision. The Grant graveyard was not far from the gates so the guards could always keep watch over the sacred area, which meant she could go there without excessive fear. The large cross carved of the strongest oak tree stood larger than any others.

Laird Alexander Grant, buried in December of 1314, husband to his dearest wife Madeline, sire to twins James (Jamie) and John (Jake), Kyla, Connor, Elizabeth, and Maeve.

She loved how he had insisted she not be identified as an adopted daughter. Her hand went to the fold in her skirt where she carried the small piece of plaid every day. She'd taken a swatch of her sire's favorite plaid and saved it as a memory of him. Before long, she found herself carrying it with her everywhere she went. She'd sewn folds in every one of her skirts so she would always have that small piece of her father with her.

Her mind often turned to her parents, Maddie and Alex Grant. The clan had lost her mother many years ago, but it had not yet been a year since the loss of her sire last Yuletide. She hadn't accepted his death yet. She'd barely accepted losing her mother, but losing her beloved Da was too much to handle. Each morning, she woke still expecting to hear his booming voice reach her from somewhere in the castle. Each morning, the grief hit her anew when he was not there.

The crisp air blew stray hairs away from her face, and she watched the leaves on the ground swirling at her feet, thinking of her mother's love for the patterns they made.

Memories of her parents filled her heart.

Her mother: *Maeve, treasure these small moments in the seasons. Each has its own special gifts. For autumn, it is the colors that dance in my heart and make me smile whenever I step outside the castle walls. The yellows and golds, the deep reds and rich greens. How beautiful the forest is at this time of year.*

Her father: *Maeve, I know ye miss yer mother as I do, but ye must set yer eyes ahead of ye. I wish ye would find yerself a husband before I pass on. Ye need someone to take care of ye.*

She'd asked him a question she nearly regretted. *Have ye moved on, Papa?*

Ye know I have no', but 'tis different for ye. Maddie is my heart, my love for my entire life. We are yer parents. 'Tis a different bond. Find the keeper of yer heart. Someday ye will. Promise me ye will no' turn him away when he comes for ye.

She glanced back at the group of guards chatting near the gates of the curtain wall. Jamie, Connor, Loki, Kenzie, Finlay MacNichol, and Maitland.

The only Menzie in the group, and he stood out to her above the others.

Was Maitland the keeper of her heart? He had been the one who rescued her when she'd fallen in the cold rain, carrying her inside the keep. He'd helped her in the orchard yesterday. But any Grant would do as much for her.

And he'd kissed her. Aye, he was the only one to do that.

She took a few steps to stroll among the many graves, heading toward the bubbling stream not far away. When she was certain the men would not hear her, she began to ask her questions.

"Papa, can I trust him with my secret? What will happen when he learns my fault?"

As if answering her, a warmth washed through her with the words "Trust him."

How she wished she knew that message had truly come from her father. Then she would trust Maitland, love him with all her heart. Indeed, she thought she might already. Last eve, she fell asleep with memories of how wonderful it had felt to be in his arms.

But how would Maitland react when he knew the truth?

Footsteps approached her from behind, and Kyla's voice reached her. "Ye are tormented, wee sister."

Maeve turned to her. Kyla carried the beauty of their father in her face and the beauty of their mother in her heart. "I am a wee bit."

"Ye can trust him, Maeve. 'Tis no' as bad a secret as ye think it is."

"Will it never go away, Kyla? The darkness. The nightmares." Her tears spilled from her eyes as if they'd been stored up for decades.

"It may not, but it could. Sleeping with Finlay makes me feel safer. Ye never slept in Papa's chamber once ye grew old enough to think on finding a lad of yer own. If ye marry, yer husband could send yer fears away for good."

She wished to believe Kyla, wished to believe that it were possible that someone could make all her troubles leave her, but what if it didn't happen? What if she married someone—perhaps Maitland—and things got worse?

Kyla gathered her in her arms and hugged her tight. "I canno' make a decision for ye, but I wish ye would trust Maitland. He's a fine man. I know ye have feelings for him, Maeve, and Papa would be pleased to see ye marry him. Mama always loved Maitland, so she would approve as much. I wish they were here for ye, but they are no', so ye must trust yer heart."

Everything Kyla said was true. She couldn't disagree with a word of it. She sighed. Perhaps it was herself she needed to trust, as much as Maitland.

Kyla let her go. "I must return, but please think on it while ye are taking yer daily stroll."

"I will, dear sister. You are surely wiser than I. Thank you."

Kyla returned to the castle, and Maeve made her way over to her favorite resting spot, a boulder near the stream. In the summer, she would remove her hose and wiggle her toes in the cool water. But not today.

She sat down and drew her legs up to her chest, resting her chin on her knees. How she wished she knew what had happened to her when she was a bairn. Something from that time must be the cause of all this, and if she could only discover it, she might conquer it and all her nightmares would go away.

But she had no memory of the time when she lived with Hew, the evil bastard. Her memories began only after dear Aline had saved her by bringing her to Clan Grant. Those who were there at the time told her she'd climbed onto Alex Grant's lap at the age of three and never left it.

Her memories of her father's lap probably began from the age of five or six. Whenever she was having a difficult day, he would sit nearby and pat his lap, indicating that she was welcome to join him.

And she always did. She would climb onto his lap and lean back against him, his warmth wrapping around her like the thickest plaid. Her thumb often ended up in her mouth, so she was told, but that part she didn't recall.

Her mother used to say that her father would sit with her in his lap even after she fell asleep, conducting his meetings with his guards while she slept, oblivious to all that went on around her.

The world always looked better from Alex Grant's lap, his large hand protecting her from all the evils of the world, no one daring to move her.

No Hew, no other bad men in the world. No guards with evil grins.

But even though she had no memory of those men who lived with Hew, they were in the darkness that often came to her in the middle of the night, reaching out for her from underneath her bed or from under Elizabeth's bed, or from the darkest corner in their bedchamber. They had to be what caused her nightmares. What else could it be?

When she was young, she would scream and run as fast as she could to her parents' bedchamber, standing at the side of the bed with tears blurring her vision until a pair of large hands lifted her and settled her between Alex and Maddie.

The safest place in all of Scotland.

That place smelled of pine and cinnamon and a sweetness that didn't exist anywhere else.

Over the years, the running had stopped, but the screaming had not.

At nearly four decades, Maeve still screamed at least once a fortnight. Screamed and struggled with an invisible monster, swinging her fists to stop her tormentor.

But her parents were never there to console her anymore. Now Kyla came to awaken her from her nightmare.

She'd never be able to marry anyone or move away from Kyla.

If no one awakened her, she'd surely die of fright.

At the scuff of footsteps through fallen leaves, she glanced over her shoulder. Maitland was coming her way, and she had to admit that a sweet tingle began in her belly. Directly at her—to see her! Or so she hoped. Changing her position to make sure she sat like a lady, she waved to him, and he broke out in a wide smile, returning her wave. "'Tis a lovely day, my lady. Would ye like to go for a stroll with me?"

Nodding, she stood as soon as he was near, smoothing the fine wrinkles in her skirt, wishing she'd been more careful to keep it tidy, but she could not worry about it now.

Maitland, the man who was stealing her heart, stood in front of her. "I asked Jamie if he minded if we kept company together. He actually pushed me in yer direction."

She giggled at that. "I doubt he pushed you, but I do believe he wishes I'd find someone." She blushed at the implication of her statement. "Forgive me. I did not mean to imply…"

He held his hand up. "Dinnae worry. I dinnae take any meaning from yer statement. Tell me, which season do ye like the best? Autumn?" He took her hand, and they headed down the path that would take them away from the curtain wall. Not far away, a few mounted guards were headed out on their daily patrol to make sure Grant land was free of reivers and marauders.

And English these days.

"I prefer Yuletide. We used to decorate the hall with greenery, and we loved the feasting and the gifts. Loki comes every year with packages and presents, which the wee ones love. Which season is your favorite?"

"Springtime. New beginnings. Fresh buds on the trees. The promise of warmth coming soon." He peered at her. "Ye looked quite pensive on the boulder. Something ye'd like to share? Sometimes talking about something helps ye find yer way out of the murkiness."

"It is quite murky. I do not recall the earliest pieces of my life, and I wish I did. I am forever searching for the cause of my nightmares, but I've never unearthed even the smallest clue. Now, I've had something similar in the light of day, and it frightens me. If I could recall what happened, would I be worse off or better? Would the nightmares worsen or improve?"

They heard the sound of approaching horse hooves, so they both looked to see who was approaching the castle. Maitland stepped closer to Maeve and released her hand so he could set his at the small of her back, a small intimacy she liked. It did indeed make her feel safer with the approach of unknown riders.

"Henry, what is it?" Maitland called as the rider drew near, another guard coming behind him.

Maeve took it as a good sign that he knew the other man. Or was it?

"My lord, yer mother has taken ill. Yer sire asks for yer return."

"She is alive? Was she hurt or is it the fever?"

"She is alive, taken to her bed. A fever of unknown origin. Yer father asks for yer return immediately. We are to escort ye home."

"I will be ready in less than half the hour. Ye

may go inside for a quick repast while I gather my belongings."

Maitland turned to her, and she could see the worry in his eyes. The man had lost his wife, so he knew grief well.

She reached up to pat his arm. "I'm so sorry, Maitland. I pray you find her healing."

"I apologize for cutting this short, but I must go and go quickly. If ye'd like, ye are welcome to ride with me."

Maeve started at the thought of joining him on his journey, and her instincts took over. "Oh, nay. Please do not be offended, but nay."

He frowned, and she nearly relented because she knew she'd caused that expression. She had to make him understand. "Maitland, I've never left Grant land."

The confusion in his gaze was clear. "Ye mentioned this before, but I thought ye meant ye'd never lived away from Grant land."

She shook her head enough to hide her embarrassment. "Nay. I've never left. Once I was brought here, I liked it so much that I swore I'd never leave. I believe I visited Ramsay land when I was verra young, but I have no memory of it. I refused to leave after I turned six summers."

There went her chance of building a family with Maitland. She could see it in his eyes, but he recovered quickly.

"Well, I look forward to our next meeting." He kissed her cheek and ushered her back to the curtain wall, their conversation ended.

She understood. What did one say to a recluse?

CHAPTER FIVE

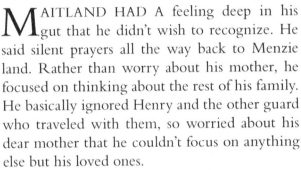

MAITLAND HAD A feeling deep in his gut that he didn't wish to recognize. He said silent prayers all the way back to Menzie land. Rather than worry about his mother, he focused on thinking about the rest of his family. He basically ignored Henry and the other guard who traveled with them, so worried about his dear mother that he couldn't focus on anything else but his loved ones.

Tad had been given the title of chieftain by their sire, Drew, who'd had more and more difficulty moving about with a bad hip. Their father had decided it was better to have Tad be the active chieftain, and he could assist him in learning his duties of taking care of the clan. Tad had married Ada, also part of the Menzie clan, and they had two lads, Wiley, five winters old, and Quillan, known affectionately as just Q, who was three winters.

The lads were as wild as any lads could be, so Maitland took them into the woods often just to let them get rid of their need to run and act like wild animals. He adored the boys and enjoyed his time with them more than he ever expected.

Which was why losing Nesta when she was with child hurt more than he'd ever thought possible.

Tomag, two years younger than Tad, was Tad's second-in-command. As his second, he had taken over the training of their men to be excellent swordsmen, hunters, and guards. Their archers had been trained by Uncle Logan, his mother's brother.

Elyse, his only sister, was the eldest, but she'd married a fine man in the Drummond clan, so she spent most of her time there.

Maitland had been born five years after Tomag. Since he had no formal title, he had decided to join the patrols that helped defend Scotland's territories from the English.

It also helped him to forget his pain.

He'd met Nesta when he'd traveled to visit his cousins. She was a member of the Drummond clan. He liked her fire and her sense of humor. They'd married a year after meeting, and she'd moved to Clan Menzie with Maitland.

It was on a trip to visit Drummond land when they'd been kidnapped and thrown into a dungeon. He'd never known their captors' identities. They'd worn no plaids nor clan colors, most surely by design. One of them had shoved a bag over Maitland's head, and they knocked him out so he had no idea where they were taken or how far they'd gone. He'd woken alone in a cell.

His captors spoke like the English and were

searching for news about the Ramsay women, though he'd never understood the reason for the constant questions. No matter the reason, they'd learned nothing at all from him or Nesta. The Menzie clan had nothing to hide other than strategic work they did with their guards and warriors, and no one had asked about that. All the questions were about the number of females on Ramsay land and whether or not they were married.

It had been most odd, but he gave them nothing.

But they'd killed his pregnant wife. That had left him with an unfulfilled need for revenge. That need, and his need to protect other women in danger, fueled everything he did now. He vowed to protect all the women of his clan and their allies—the Drummonds, the Ramsays, the Grants, the Camerons, and the Mathesons. And vowed that if he ever discovered the identity of his captors, he would make sure they felt the full extent of his own pain.

Being part of the patrol had been a strategic decision driven by that need for revenge. The more he traveled, the better the chance he'd have of finding the bastards.

Five years gone, and he'd never found them. Would he ever?

The trio neared Menzie land, and Maitland was pleased to see a group of Menzie plaids approaching them on horseback, his eldest brother in the lead. Tomag rode with him, and both wore serious expressions. He didn't like that. Tomag was a jokester at heart and almost always had a smile on his face. But if their mother were severely ill, they would be by her bedside, surely.

"Tad, how is Mama?"

"Mama will heal, I believe. Aunt Brenna arrived last eve with Uncle Logan, and Uncle Micheil arrived today. Having her brothers here has perked Mama up," Tomag said.

Tad added, "And having Aunt Brenna here perked me up. Mama is already improving. She had a fever that would no' break. Aunt Brenna is mixing potions and keeping a close eye on her."

"I'm glad to hear it. I canno' wait to see her." He hadn't been home in a while because of his patrol duties, so he was due. His plan had been to travel to Grant land, spend a few days there, then return home for Yule. The news about his mother had simply brought him home a day or two early.

They made their way back to the stables, and the stable lads came out to take care of the horses. He dismounted and found himself in a giant bear hug that he couldn't break if he wanted to.

"Uncle Micheil, fare thee well?"

"Of course I am well."

"Aunt Diana?"

"As beautiful as ever. And so are all our bairns and grandbairns." Uncle Micheil stepped back and clasped his shoulders. "I hear ye are doing a fine job for King Robert, sending the English bastards back where they belong. Keep doing so, will ye no'? The fact that they dared to approach Cameron Castle shocks me. They need to stay in the Borderlands."

"I do my best. We sent a few groups running

south with their tails lowered." Uncle Micheil was the tallest of the three brothers and the broadest in the shoulders too. Quade had been nearly as tall as Micheil, and both towered over Logan, whose power was in his shoulders and his sword. He may have been shorter than his brothers, but he looked more powerful because of his swordsman's muscles and stance.

And his intellect. Uncle Logan had proven time and time again to be a crafty old Scotsman. Few dared to cross him. He joined the group outside the stable now.

"Uncle Logan, always a pleasure. I'm sure Mama is pleased to see ye two together."

"She's improving, and I'm sure 'tis my presence that pleases her." His smug look told Maitland exactly what he was about. The two brothers were competitive even when it came to their only sister's affection. "Ye know Lina always loved me best."

Uncle Micheil gave his brother a shove. "Forget it, old man. I'll not take the bait ye are throwing at me. Ye are too old to be fighting with." That brought a snort from Uncle Logan.

The group made their way into the great hall, and as soon as the doors opened, they were set upon by two lads. "Uncle Maitland, ye are home," Wiley said, throwing himself at Maitland.

Q said, "Are ye 'taying dis time?" At the age of three, Q was still practicing his speech. Maitland had trouble understanding him at times, but once he realized that many of his words started with 'd' or 't' it became easier. And if Maitland didn't understand, Wiley did. The two began to pull and tug at him, so he picked each of them up separately, wrapping an arm around each lad's waist and turning them sideways so he had one on each side, their legs kicking freely. Then he bounced as he walked, both lads squealing and yelling, trying to break his grip, but he didn't let up until he found a soft pile of pillows near the hearth. He tossed the two onto the heap with a growl, the two overcome with endless laughter as they struggled to get up and get back to their uncle.

A voice caught him from above. "That must be my youngest son who has finally arrived. No one else makes the lads giggle like that. Come visit me, Maitland!" His mother's voice carried over the balcony from the bedchamber she shared with his sire. "I'd recognize yer growl anywhere."

"I'm coming, Mama. As soon as these two wild animals stop attacking me." Wiley came at him again so he tipped him upside down as he shrieked, then turned him before tossing him back on the pillows. Q did the same, mimicking exactly what his brother had done, so he treated him the same, though a bit more gently.

"Lads," Tad said. "Leave Uncle Maitland be for now. He wishes to see Grandmama. Go help Cook by picking some apples from the orchard out back. Mayhap she'll make ye some fruit tarts if ye find a few."

"I doeing," Q said, meaning *going*. His brother was already halfway to the door. The two disappeared, their laughter echoing behind them.

Maitland grabbed an ale, downed it quickly, then made his way up the staircase, a part of him dreading what he'd find in his mother's bedchamber.

He could not lose his mother right now. He was not ready for that. He climbed slowly, thinking of what he might tell his mother that would cheer her. His thoughts went to Maeve, to the fact that he was actually having feelings for a woman again. And to the halo he'd seen around her head.

Had he imagined it?

As he approached the chamber door, he steeled himself to contain any expression of surprise or distress that might come from her appearance. His mother was one of the most beautiful women he knew. She still was, even though her hair had turned as white as a fresh snowfall on the side of a hill, glittering in the sun. He swore she had sparkles in her hair, but he'd looked up close and never found any.

Aunt Brenna stepped out and gave him a swift hug as he approached the door, then bussed his cheek. "Yer mother has been waiting for ye to arrive. Do no' worry, she's no' ready to leave this world yet. She's coming along nicely from a fever that forced her to slow down." She added in a whisper, "She may need to slow down a wee bit more. Leave the lads to ye men, if they're going to be wild."

"I heard that, Brenna. I can still handle my grandsons. I need more of them."

Maitland laughed and said, "Many thanks, Aunt

Brenna, for all ye have done. We all know ye are the best."

"Hush now, Maitland. My sister Jennie is just as skilled. I'll leave ye and yer mother to talk. Avelina needs more broth. I'll find her some." She headed down the stairs and toward the kitchens.

Maitland stepped into the chamber, not surprised to smell various aromas from the many potions and ointments his aunt brought along. His mother surprised him more. She looked radiant.

"Mama, ye look lovely as ever." He bent down to kiss her cheek, and she patted a spot on the bed next to her. She was propped with many pillows, and while she did look wonderful, up close he caught the paleness of her skin and the shadows under her eyes, signs of exactly how ill she'd been.

"Many thanks to ye, Maitland. I was hoping ye would come home." She squeezed his hand. "I canno' explain it, but for some reason, I felt we needed ye."

"I'm glad ye sent for me. I was on my way home anyway but had stopped for a visit with Clan Grant, so not on patrol. We are done until after Yule."

"And how are the Grants? Tell me all about them." She looked at him knowingly. "I think ye have yer eye on someone."

He didn't ask how she knew, but instead considered how much to reveal. His mother had a reputation as a seer and had been the keeper of the sapphire sword for many years. She had passed it on to Alexander Grant's great-grandson, John Grant, who had pledged to guard the valuable weapon as it deserved to be.

Maitland knew there was no purpose in hiding his feelings from his mother. She would figure it all out anyway.

"I enjoyed my time with Connor and Jamie and also spent some time with Finlay, but I spent more time with Maeve."

"Maeve? The youngest lass of Alex and Maddie? Wonderful!" Her eyes lit up, letting him know he'd made the right decision to tell all. "She is older. Probably about the same age as ye are."

"Aye. Unlike me, she's never married. She took a fall in the rain, and I carried her inside. While I was helping her, the oddest thing happened. I wished to ask ye about it if ye promise no' to tell another soul." If either of his brothers ever heard his words, they'd tease him for days. Or years.

"Go ahead, Maitland. Ye have my word." She folded her hands in her lap, a move that always told him he had her full attention.

"I carried her into the healing chamber while Jamie fetched Gracie. The strangest thing happened, and I know no' what to think of it." He glanced over his shoulder to make sure no one had entered the chamber. No one had, but he paused to close the door to keep prying ears away. "When I laid her down on the pallet, there was a golden glow around her head. What do ye make of it, Mama?" He returned to his seat on the bed and waited for his mother's response.

"Was she conscious?"

"Nay. She had a nasty bump on her head from the fall, and it must have knocked her out. She came to a short time later, but she hadn't awakened yet when the glow appeared."

"How long did it last? Did anyone else notice it, then or later?"

"Nay, when Gracie opened the door, it disappeared."

"Truly. Hmmm. That is a puzzle. I've never seen anything like it, at least no' around someone's head, but I've noticed odd glows in other places."

"And?"

"And to me it means that Heaven above has come to assist in whatever is taking place."

"Mama, she looked like..." He paused to look over his shoulder again then whispered, "...an angel."

His mother's face lit up. "Oh, Maitland. Ye've finally found her."

He arched a brow. "What do ye mean?"

She reached for his hand and squeezed it. "That tells me she is yer soulmate. Please dinnae walk away from her. Spend more time with her at the verra least. Follow the guidance the angels have sent ye. If ye were the only one who saw the golden aura, then 'twas meant for yer eyes only."

"The angels have sent me guidance? I dinnae understand."

"I believe that we all have guiding angels. They do their best to guide us along our path, but 'tis our job to listen and follow that path. Some people need more nudging than others."

"So what does this mean for me?"

"It means ye were nudged. Ye were ignoring yer guiding angel, so she gave ye a stronger sign. One ye canno' ignore. Maeve is for ye to marry. Ye could have a bairn waiting to be born. Ye must listen to the message, Maitland. Please."

The door opened and hit the wall with a bang. His mother rolled her eyes. "Logan, do what ye wish to the doors in yer house, but please leave mine alone. In this house, we knock before we enter someone's bedchamber."

He gave his sister a lopsided grin and shrugged. "Sorry. Ye look much better, Lina. Maitland healed ye, aye?"

She smiled at him. "Aye, my youngest is here. All is right with the world."

An uneasy feeling crept across Maitland, something he didn't like at all.

Everything was not right with the world, though he couldn't say what it might be. Did it have aught to do with Maeve? Would he have to listen to a guiding angel to find out?

CHAPTER SIX

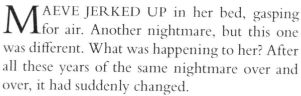

MAEVE JERKED UP in her bed, gasping for air. Another nightmare, but this one was different. What was happening to her? After all these years of the same nightmare over and over, it had suddenly changed.

She'd seen a face.

She looked for Kyla, who was always at her bedside when she woke. Her sister wasn't there.

Kyla hadn't come.

Kyla always came, drawn either by Maeve's screams or some sixth sense for Maeve's troubles. It was Kyla who woke her. This time Maeve had woken on her own.

Where was her sister? Deciding not to wait, she climbed out of bed and found her plaid, wrapping it over her shoulders and hugging it around her middle. She tiptoed out of her bedchamber and down the stairs.

No one was about, but she had to think. That had not been her normal dream. She'd seen someone this time, though no one she recognized. He had the look of evil about him—a sneer on his face and hate in his eyes.

She shivered, then grabbed a woolen blanket to place over her lap as she took a chair in front of the hearth, willing herself to calm down.

The sound of feet coming down a passageway from one of the towers caught her attention. Maisie hurried across the cold stone surface and fell into a chair next to Maeve with a plop.

"Did you have the nightmare again?" the other woman asked.

"Aye. I saw a face this time." Maisie and Morna, Aline's sisters, had been kept in the same castle where Maeve had been found. They'd all been rescued together, according to the story. Hew, the man who'd stolen them from their homes, was dead and would never bother them again, but the castle had held other people since then.

According to the story Maeve had heard, she and Morna, close to the same age, had been minded in the castle by a woman who'd had her own bairn. Morna said she had no nightmares and, like Maeve, had no memories of their time there.

Maisie, who was three years older than Maeve, had been plagued by nightmares the same as Maeve over the years. She said the dreams had eased since her marriage, though they still came. Whenever she awakened from a nightmare, she would roll into his warm embrace and everything disappeared.

Maisie's voice came out in a low whisper now. "This was different."

Had they had the same dream? Maeve had to know. "Was it a face?"

Maisie nodded, paling enough that Maeve noticed it even in the dark of night. "It was Hew." Maisie bolted out of her chair and threw some firewood into the hearth, the crackle of the fresh wood warming Maeve's cheeks.

"Was it? You are certain?"

Maisie sighed. "It was Hew, but it wasn't Hew. He looked the same but different. I don't understand."

Maeve said, "I wish I had some memories of him."

"Nay, you do not. None of them are pleasant. He was a cruel man, and so were the men who were with him."

"But did they not die? Didn't Jake kill Hew?"

"Aye. Most of them are dead or fled after the Grants arrived. Maeve, why are we both having the same dream? Do you recall anything else about yours?"

"Nay. Just…" Maeve didn't know exactly how to express what she was feeling.

"What? Please tell me what you are thinking. We're in this together, Maeve."

Maisie was right, so she did her best to find the words.

"Impending doom. It's as though something is about to happen, and it will be bad."

Truly bad. Worse than she wished to admit. But what did it mean?

Maitland stayed another day before heading back to Grant land. He could simply stay through

Yule—he'd planned to come here for the festive season anyway—but he had unfinished business back at Grant Castle. He wanted to take Maeve a Yuletide gift, and he knew in his heart his mother was right. He and Maeve belonged together. They could work with Maeve's disinclination to leave Grant land.

And now that he'd acknowledged his feelings for her, he did not want to delay. Neither of them were young. Which meant they didn't have much time to waste second-guessing or playing coy. And they knew what to expect out of life.

Not much.

Maitland sat on a large boulder at the Menzie archery field, an old shield fashioned into a target on a post a short distance away. He'd been working with the lads on learning to use their slings. Q was perhaps a wee bit young yet—he'd managed to hit himself with his stones as often as the target. But they all knew the story of Loki and how he'd been adopted by Brodie Grant after they found him and that he'd fought in the Battle of Largs using his sling and knocked out a few Norsemen.

Wiley let fly a stone three times and hit the target once. "Why am I missing?"

Q said, "Do dat way, Wi." He'd shortened his brother's name, just as Wiley had shortened his when he hadn't been able to say *Quillan*.

"Do what?" Maitland asked Q.

Wiley shook his head. "Not *do*. he said *go*. 'Go that way.' He wants me to try from this side."

Maitland glanced over at Q, who was grinning

and nodding. The two had the same blond hair that carried a wee bit of wave when the wind messed it up. And they understood each other better than anyone. Like most brothers, Maitland reckoned.

"I'll try it, Q," Wiley said.

Sure enough, Wiley hit two out of three, and Q squealed with delight. "He did it!"

"Now ye try, Q."

Q gave it his best effort, but his face fell when he missed the target completely with all three stones.

Hoofbeats caught Maitland's attention, and he was surprised to see an unexpected trio approaching. Loki Grant tied his horse to a nearby tree and dismounted, his son Lucas and adopted son Kenzie just behind him.

Loki raised a hand in greeting to Maitland, then called out to the boys. "Let me have a look at those weapons ye are using, lads. Mayhap I have finer ones for ye."

Maitland rose to greet his friend. Though not of the same blood, anyone from Grant land felt like family to him. "Loki, so pleased to see ye, but what brings ye here?"

"We're just passing through. The lads and I always head to Ayr and Edinburgh just before Yule to search out any more lads living in crates like I did. We hope ye would oblige us with warm beds and good food for the night. We'll be moving on in the morn."

Tad came along behind the three. "The others who came with ye are already being fed. Ye are always welcome here, Loki. These are my lads, Wiley and Quillan, though we call him Q. They've been doing their best to improve their skills with their slings."

"Many thanks to ye, Tad." Loki turned to the boys and said, "Here, lads. Allow me to inspect yer slings. Mayhap Lucas has a couple spares for ye too. Not to say yers aren't good, but we're known for making the best in the land."

Wiley brought his over and said, "Greetings to ye, my lord."

Loki smiled. "Nay lord here. Just call me Loki. And this is Lucas and Kenzie. We all use slings."

Q looked up at Loki and asked, "'Ten ye hep us, peez?"

Loki ruffled Q's hair and said, "I'd love to. Will ye promise me an apple from yer orchard in return?"

"We already picked some," Wiley said. "Cook is making apple tarts for supper. Ye can have two."

"Many thanks to ye. Maitland made ye a fine sling, but try these two that Lucas has with him. He and Kenzie will teach ye the way to shoot them."

Maitland, Loki, and Tad stood back and watched the lads practice with their new slings, cheering when they hit the target.

"Maitland, ye've been on patrol, I hear. Anything ye wish to share about yer travels?" Loki asked, crossing his arms as he watched the lads.

"Not much. The English bastards have been coming much farther north and no one likes it, but we managed to send many of them back. Or bury them."

Loki laughed. "'Tis the best place for them in the Highlands. Deep in the ground."

"Have ye seen any along yer journey?" Maitland asked.

"Nay, but we travel quickly. I only bring four others with us, so we are less than ten. And I take advantage of my friendships for shelter at night. These bones are too old to enjoy sleeping on the ground anymore. I prefer a pallet anywhere inside. I dinnae need a soft bed, just a pallet inside away from the cold of winter." He wore a thick mantle with a long scarf. "We often find a few lads and bring them home, but they are no' used to the cold Highland nights either. I am grateful for yer hospitality, Menzies."

"Think naught of it. We always enjoy seeing ye," Maitland said.

Wiley ran over to stand in front of Loki, his hand full of small stones. "Lucas gave us each a sack to carry our stones in, but he also said to always keep some to stop bad men who might be taking us away or chasing us. He said to ask ye how ye did it."

Tad chuckled along with his brother, and Loki asked, "Lucas is telling tales again, aye?"

Lucas said, "Da, 'tis a great story. Tell them how ye made the big, mean Norseman scream like a wee bairn."

Q and Wiley waited patiently, their faces full of anticipation.

"'Tis a fine secret I'll tell ye, laddies." The tall man knelt down so he was at their level.

"What is the secret?" Wiley asked.

"What secwet?" Q mimicked.

"Ye put the stones in the villain's shoes while they are sleeping. Then they canno' chase ye."

The two boys chuckled with glee and a hint of troublemaking.

"What did he do?" Wiley asked.

"What do?" Q repeated.

Loki leaned over and whispered, "A mean old Norseman I was following holed up in an abandoned house for the night. I knew I'd need to follow him when he left, but I needed to rest too. So after he went to sleep, I snuck over and put stones in his shoes. When the surly pig-nut put them on, he cursed and swore and yelled for half the hour. And I knew he was leaving so I followed him. Then I knew where he was going."

Wiley looked at Q and said, "We must fill our sacks."

The two ran off to complete their task, but Tad called out, "Ye're never to do that to yer parents or yer uncles!"

Loki laughed as the boys ran off, then his expression turned more serious. "Have ye had much problem with reivers? We haven't seen any about nor heard much news of trouble. Any insight from either of ye? We always run into marauders or reivers trying to steal sheep."

"I dinnae see any either," Maitland said. "And I agree with ye. Something is odd about that."

What the hell was going on?

CHAPTER SEVEN

M AEVE SEARCHED THE ground of the orchard for any last pieces of fruit, but there weren't many left. The day was closing, and she could feel the beginnings of a change in the winds, so she hurried her tasks to get back inside in case of a storm.

She had a guard with her, and the gates were manned by two guards, as always, so she'd dared to return to the outer orchard, in defiance of her thudding heart. She'd done it once, which meant she could do it again, with reasonable precautions. She was always aware of where her guard was, always listened for anyone approaching, always made sure the gate guards were within hailing distance. And she'd been fine.

She *could* conquer her fears, she thought proudly.

On the way back, she stopped at her mother's and father's graves, saying a quiet prayer for the Lord to keep them both in His arms.

Just as she stepped inside the curtain wall, the sound of hooves reached her ears. She stopped to see who it was before she headed to the stables to leave a few apples in the basket for the stable lads and the horses. To her delight, it was Maitland.

She'd thought about him many times over the few days he'd been gone, thought about the kiss they'd shared and how much she'd enjoyed it. He was a fine man with nice manners, and he was as handsome as anyone could be in her eyes. His bright smile lit up her insides.

But she couldn't forget what she'd told him. That she'd never marry because she could never leave Grant land. How she wished he would consider living here with her, but knowing how much he liked to patrol the land made her reconsider that possibility.

She knew it to be the truth that she could never leave. She'd not had much desire to leave Grant land in the last three decades of her life, and even the prospect of a husband and family of her own hadn't been enough to entice her away. Oh, she'd been told she'd gone to Ramsay land and Cameron land a few times when she was young, and she held vague memories of it, but she usually rode on her father's lap on his big warhorse. No man would dare cross Midnight or Alexander Grant.

But as time passed, her father only left for battle, and she sat in the keep awaiting his safe return. She often wondered why she'd clung to her parents so. Kyla went wherever Finlay went, and Elizabeth and Gil moved back and forth between Castle Grant and Castle Curanta all the time. But Finlay had always lived at Clan Grant so this was home to both of them.

Maitland would probably prefer to live on Menzie land. Or was he meant to be a constant traveler like Logan Ramsay? Perhaps she should try broaching the subject with him if the opportunity ever arose.

Aline, bless her soul, had told her it was because of their life during the time they were with Hew. She had spent her early years living in constant fear. She'd suggested that Maeve held that fear inside her, unable to let it go. If she couldn't remember that life, she couldn't release the fear it had instilled in her.

Since she'd never been interested in a man, staying close to her family had never been an issue.

Maeve greeted Maitland as soon as he came through the gate of the curtain wall. "Welcome, Maitland. I am pleased you have come back. I was not certain if you planned to or not. How does your mother fare?"

He dismounted and approached her, kissing her cheek, making Maeve smile. "It's good to be back and to see ye again, Maeve. Mama is well, I'm happy to say. It's partly due to her that I'm here."

"I want to hear your news. I'll join you in the hall after I deliver these apples to the stable. Would your mount enjoy a treat?"

"No doubt he would. But first…" Maitland reached to the back of his horse and freed a parcel wrapped in oil cloth. "Here. I brought ye a gift. A new basket for ye. I noticed yer other one had grown a bit worn."

She took the gift in hand and studied it. A

fine red ribbon had been woven into the basket around the top. "Maitland, it's beautiful. I love it. Many thanks to you."

A few minutes later, both her apples and Maitland's horse were safely in the stable, and she strolled with him up to the hall. "Tell me what you found at home. Was your mother terribly ill?"

"Something gave her the fever, but one of my aunts came to tend her. She was much better when I arrived and in no danger."

"And ye fare well?"

"Verra well, but I missed ye, Maeve. I enjoy yer company, and I wished to return to ye. And maybe share another kiss, if ye're agreeable."

"No trouble on your journey?"

"Nay. My men thought a storm was brewing, but I'm not sure it will hit Grant land. No matter, the temperature is dropping fast, so I'm glad to be here."

"The evening meal has passed but we have extra meat pies. Mutton, I believe. Would you like one?"

"I would love one, if ye dinnae mind. My men will stay in the stables as usual, but they could use some food. We traveled quickly because of the temperature change. What have ye that I could bring to them?"

"Come with me and we'll see what Cook has left."

They entered the kitchens off the back of the hall, and Maeve was surprised to see it empty. She nearly jumped when she felt his hands on her hips. He spun her around and bent his head toward hers.

"I've been thinking of our kiss, Maeve. What say ye?"

Her answer was to tug him down until his lips melded with hers. She let out a deep sigh and parted her lips for him, enjoying the dueling of their tongues. At first, Maitland was soft and tender, but his kiss became rougher, and she found she liked it. He needed her, and she wished to fuel that need—and satisfy it. His lips left her mouth and traveled down her neck, placing light kisses that set her insides aflame. The heat traveled to her core and her women's parts, sending a tingle through her that made her shiver. She'd never experienced anything like it before.

Oh, she'd seen a man's needs, but the one who stole her maidenhead had been harsh and coarse. Even his kisses, bordering on bites, left her skin raw. She'd done her best to end their time together, but she'd been naïve, allowing things that she didn't understand, and she'd lost her maidenhead before she knew what was happening. The pain told her what he'd done.

Afterward, he'd apologized profusely, but she'd vowed to stay far away from him. That had been easy; he'd disappeared the next day, probably fearing she'd tell her father and he'd have forced the marriage.

She would have refused. The man was no villain, but she would not have enjoyed a life with him. She'd been young and foolish, and she had learned her lesson without any disastrous consequences. She hadn't traded kisses with many others since then.

And none had been as delicious as Maitland Menzie's.

The door opened and one of the serving lasses entered. "Yer pardon," she said, ducking her head. "I thought to grab an extra hunk of bread for my mother."

"Go ahead and take what ye need. We are gathering a meal for the Menzie guards."

Maitland chose a loaf of dark bread, a hunk of cheese, and three meat pies for his friends to share. There was always mead in the guards' accommodations next to the stables. They delivered the food to the men, fighting the rising wind all the way to the stable.

On the way back, Maitland took her hand and said, "Come with me. I love to go atop the curtain wall and watch a storm roll in."

"It will be here soon." Maeve tugged her mantle around her neck and tightened her scarf. "This will be a new experience for me. I usually make sure I am safe inside before a storm." New adventures weren't quite so daunting with Maitland by her side.

He took her hand and led her up the steps to the curtain wall. They found a spot to lean on to watch the weather surrounding them, an eerie sight with clouds swirling in the dusk, but a touch of sun still glowing at the western horizon. Maitland tucked her in front of him so he could keep her warm and protect her from some of the gusts, which seemed even more powerful up on the parapets. The clouds raced across the sky as the wind whistled through the forest

"There," Maitland said, pointing above them. "See how beautiful that cloud is? It's likely to bring a thunderstorm because 'tis such a large cloud, and it keeps darkening and changing its shape."

"I think it is beautiful, Maitland. The colors of the night sky are glorious."

A motion outside the wall caught the corner of her eye. "Maitland, look. Down there. Is that not a child running across the meadow?"

He peered toward the path that led into the forest and bellowed, "Come back! Get out of the storm!"

The figure didn't even slow down. Perhaps the wind had blown Maitland's words away from her. Maeve didn't recognize the young lass, whose red hair would surely be memorable.

"Who lives over there?" Maitland asked.

"No one, to my knowledge. Come, we must find her and bring her back."

Maitland didn't hesitate. They headed down the stairs and to the gate, explained to the guards where they were headed, then hurried to follow the lass's path. They nearly caught up with her at the edge of the forest, and she turned to smile at them, her hair a mass of red curls and a face full of freckles. Maeve guessed her to be around ten summers. She waved them forward but continued to run.

"Nay, come back!" Maeve yelled, fearing the girl was in danger. "You must come inside."

They chased her, but she refused to stop, only looking back to see if they were following. She didn't look frightened at all but seemed more to be enjoying a game.

"Should we go back, Maitland? She's not going to stop." She had an odd feeling the girl had a destination in mind, but Maeve had no idea what it might be. There was a small village around Grant Castle, as there was around most castles, where the clan mates grew crops and tilled the fields, but they were going away from the village, not toward it. With every step, they went deeper into the forest.

"Are there cottages this far into the woods? Where could she be going?" Maitland asked. They hurried on, not really considering stopping.

"None that I am aware of. Mama would ride out with provisions to some of the more distant cottages and huts, but she never went this way. Nor have any of my sisters when they took over the duty."

"Mayhap they have found an empty house to live in. Is that possible?"

"I think there might be two abandoned houses deep into the woods. The old healer used to live in one before she died, I've heard. But I know not if it's still standing."

"Then we follow to make sure she arrives safely. Ye'll sleep better, and so will I."

They continued, and just as the empty cottages came into view, the clouds opened up with a pelting rain, pouring down all around them. The lass squealed and ran straight into one of the old cottages.

Lightning flashed all around them, lighting up the night. The thunder was so loud it hurt her ears.

"Shall we go back?" Maitland asked. "She's inside."

Another harsh crack of loud thunder with three bolts of blinding lightning convinced her.

"Nay, we stay. We'll be struck by lightning for sure if we go out in the open."

CHAPTER EIGHT

THE LASS APPEARED in the doorway and waved them inside. "Hurry, ye're both getting soaked."

Maeve rushed inside while Maitland shielded her from the weather with his body. She appreciated his chivalry, but pulled him inside immediately behind her.

"Here," the lass said, "hang yer mantles by the hearth."

Once they removed their outer clothing, Maeve said, "Greetings to you. My name is Maeve and this is Maitland. Lass, what is your name? I've never seen you before on Grant land."

"Callie. My name is Callie. We just moved here." She helped them hang their coats and scarves on pegs near the hearth.

Maitland stomped his feet to remove as much water as he could, then moved to the hearth. He took firewood from a nearby box and arranged it carefully inside the arching stone fireplace.

Maeve glanced around. The cottage was old but clean. She could tell someone had fussed over the old stone and wood surfaces, clearing whatever dust and cobwebs might have accumulated over the years and polishing everything possible to a shine.

"This is a fine place ye live in, Callie."

Maitland lay tinder then struck his flint and steel, throwing sparks into a bit of char cloth. The golden glow in his tinder became flames on the hearth in no time at all.

"'Tis no' much, but we are happy here." The girl nodded her red mop of curls as if to confirm she was telling the truth.

The small hut was empty save for the three of them. "Where are your mama and papa?"

"They dinnae live here. I live with the sisters. They adopted me when I lost my parents to the fever a long time ago. I've always lived here with them."

Maeve thought her heart would burst open and ache for days. She identified with the lass so much. Maitland stepped up when he finished bringing the fire to life, then set his hand at the curve of Maeve's back. His support gave her the courage to continue.

"I lost my parents when I was young also." She sank into one of the two chairs by the fire, glad of its warmth.

"What happened to them?" Callie asked, fetching a blanket from a basket and handing it to Maeve. The flames cast an odd glow around her red hair.

"I do not truly know. I was taken in by a verra mean man, but if they died before that or if he killed them or simply stole me away, I cannot say.

I was rescued by two angels from Heaven, Alex and Maddie Grant, and they loved and raised me as their own."

"Do they live in that big castle?" Callie pulled a stool over and sat down in front of Maeve while Maitland took the other chair.

Maeve rubbed her hands together, thinking that she wasn't as upset being in a strange place as she would have thought. "They have both passed on, but aye, they were from Clan Grant. He was the laird. Maddie left us many years ago, but we lost Alex just last Yuletide." Her eyes teared up but didn't spill over. Crying in front of this wee lass was hardly appropriate behavior.

She decided to change the subject. "Where are your sisters?" The hut was more than livable if they'd only been here a short time. The back wall held another hearth for cooking, with a large black pot hanging from a hook over the ashes from the last fire. The hearth they sat at was on the side wall. There was a large table in front of the cooking hearth and numerous shelves on either side where cups, dishes, and utensils sat. The floor was dirt with rushes woven into a mat in the center area, and dried flowers hung from the ceiling that gave the area a fresh aroma. Baskets of fall vegetables and fruits sat on the table, ready to be turned into a meal.

Two doors flanked the front fireplace, she guessed for two bedchambers, which would share the heat of the fire through the stones of the fireplace and chimney. There was also a table with four stools around it in the center of the room.

Callie found a candle and lit it with a rush set aglow in the fire, then moved about the chamber to light up a few more. "One of the sisters makes tallow candles, so we have plenty. I prefer a bright chamber over a dark one. The sisters travel to the abbey not far away. They are usually home by dusk, but the storm probably kept them at the abbey. We have an understanding that if they ever dinnae make it home, I am to remain here until they can return."

She returned to her stool and gave a contented smile, a blanket of her own around her shoulders. "Are ye husband and wife? Like ye to sleep together? The sisters' bed, in the chamber on the right, is large enough for ye both."

Maitland opened his mouth to answer, but Maeve jumped in and said, "Aye, we sleep together." She surprised herself with that answer, but she knew she would need Maitland's heat for the night in this cold house. And she'd feel much safer if Maitland was in the same chamber with her.

He started to say something but she hushed him with a look. They could discuss it in private.

Then she realized what the lass had said, and she tipped her head back and chuckled. "Oh, those kinds of sisters. I thought you had three siblings. You mean nuns."

"Aye, they are nuns. I dinnae have any siblings. I wish I did, but I am an only child."

"We will stay with ye until the sisters return," Maitland said. "In the morning, if the storm is over, I can cut firewood for ye for another day."

Maeve's mind spun with so many questions, she didn't know which one to ask first. She wasn't worried about Maitland and their night together. They would be fine after they discussed everything. But the lass and her situation were definitely unique. She didn't wish to offend the girl, but she was puzzled about her situation. Once she settled on how to start, she said, "You said earlier that you lost your parents long ago. I'm so sorry to hear that."

"Dinnae feel badly for me. Papa and Mama are in Heaven, but I can hear Mama in my head. She talks with me all the time. She says I will live with someone else soon, that I might have some siblings too."

The lass moved over to a chest on the far wall and rustled through the contents. "Here, Lady Maeve. I think this night rail will fit ye."

"Many thanks to you, Callie. My clothes are still damp and it has been a long day, so I would like to change for bed." She followed Callie's direction into the chamber to the right.

The furnishings were spare—so minimal, in fact, that if Maeve didn't know otherwise, she'd say no one stayed there.

CHAPTER NINE

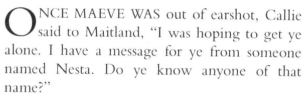

ONCE MAEVE WAS out of earshot, Callie said to Maitland, "I was hoping to get ye alone. I have a message for ye from someone named Nesta. Do ye know anyone of that name?"

Maitland's heart jumped into his throat, though he tried to maintain his usual calm demeanor. "I do know someone named Nesta. What does she say?" He didn't give away that Nesta was no longer in this world but had moved on to the next. If the lass spoke as if his wife still lived, he'd know if the lass was trying to fool him. Whether it was trickery or not, he wished to hear what the lass had to say.

Or what Nesta had to say.

"She says ye must move on. That 'twas no' yer fault what happened. Ye think she was beaten until she died, but 'tis no' the truth."

Maitland had never spoken to anyone about the guilt he carried for Nesta's death, that he believed it his own fault that she'd been beaten just a room away while he'd been helpless to act. How could this lass have any knowledge of it? She'd have been but five winters when it had happened.

Both desperate for and fearful of the answer, he forced the question from his lips. "Then what is the truth?"

"She delivered yer bairn and 'twas verra difficult for her. She said she screamed from the pain of pushing her out and again when she learned the lass had died in her womb. And then she passed on because of bleeding—her birthing blood would no' stop flowing—no' because the guards mistreated her. The midwife couldnae do anything for either mother or bairn." Callie paused and adjusted her blanket. "I feel terrible giving ye this information, Master Maitland, but my mama is next to her and says ye must hear all of this." She waited, then reached for his hand. "All will be well. Ye will have bairns but only if ye dinnae wait long. She said the perfect one for ye is in the next chamber."

Maitland could find no words to answer her. Clearly this child was a seer, gifted beyond his own mother's skills, even. The words she spoke had the weight of truth to them, which he'd learned to recognize when his mother spoke from her own special sight.

"Oh, and Mama said I must tell ye something else. The men didnae want ye. They wanted yer bairn. They wished to sell it."

Maitland pondered this statement, wondering if it could indeed be the truth. He'd heard of people who claimed to speak with the dead, but this was far beyond that.

He set aside the question of where Callie's information came from and considered the situation. Had Nesta delivered the bairn and not died from a beating? Was her death due to bleeding?

Had the men wanted the bairn and not them? Many years ago, men had been running something called the Channel of Dubh. They'd been stealing bairns to sell, bairns of all ages. They'd tried to sell Kenzie and Steenie and many others. He'd have to ask Connor more about those circumstances, since he'd been involved with stopping the cruel scheme. But it did answer some of his questions about that time—why they'd been taken in the first place, the interrogation topics, and why Nesta had been their captors' focus.

Maeve stepped out of the chamber looking every bit the angel, with the night rail floating around her and her golden hair falling halfway down her back. Maitland had to force himself not to stare at her.

She apologized and said, "I had to let my hair down to dry. I know it is not proper. Mama always said to dry my hair before I went to bed."

"Maeve, yer hair is lovely as are ye. But the best part of ye is yer big heart."

She blushed and hurried back to the hearth, grabbing the blanket she had been using before. "'Tis chilly in there." She glanced at Maitland and frowned. "You look like you've seen a ghost, Maitland. Are you all right?"

"Aye, I'm fine." He reached for Maeve's hand and cocooned it in his own two. "Ye are cold."

The words he'd just heard reverberated in his mind. He knew they'd been the truth: Maeve was the one for him. And then he recalled something else Callie had said, which he'd nearly missed amongst all the other revelations.

Callie had said that they could still have bairns if they did not wait. He and Maeve. He was overcome with emotion he hadn't expected. Joy. The heavens had just told him he was free to love Maeve the way he wished.

He could love Maeve, marry her, and have a family with her. There would be no guilt about betraying Nesta if she was watching from above. In fact, Nesta herself had said it was time to move on.

Would Maeve accept his love, though? Would she accept him as her husband?

Callie said, "He dinnae see a ghost, but he did speak with one. Yer turn will come soon, Lady Maeve."

"My turn? What is she talking about, Maitland?"

"Maitland, may I speak with Lady Maeve alone, please?" Callie asked.

He knew that meant Callie had a message for Maeve, and he would not interfere. "I'll tell ye later, Maeve. I'll take care of the fire, then see myself to bed. I hope ye will join me after ye have a wee chat with Callie." He needed to think on all he'd just heard. He kissed her forehead and said, "Come to bed when ye are ready, love."

Love was overwhelming him. But one recurrent thought would not let go.

Was it truly time for him to marry again?

Maeve looked at Callie. "What did you say to him? He looks confused, muddled."

"I had a message for him just like I have a message for ye, Lady Maeve. Please sit down and warm yerself by the fire."

Maeve wrapped her blanket around her shoulders and pulled her chair closer to the fireplace, sighing as warmth moved through her. "I don't understand, Callie. How can you have a message for me?"

"Someone who is with my mama has a message for ye. He says to listen carefully."

Maeve didn't know what to say. Were Callie's communications with her mother all in her mind, or did they truly have some kind of connection that let Callie hear those who'd gone beyond the grave? She was not sure whether to trust the lass or not, but curiosity made her speak.

"Go ahead, Callie. Who is this person?"

"He says to tell ye that Maitland will safeguard yer heart. That ye must get over yer fears and trust him."

She'd love to believe her words, but she couldn't without knowing who they came from, if it really was from someone who'd passed on. "Who is speaking, Callie?"

"He says his name is Alexander. He's yer father."

Her heart skipped a beat, but then she reminded herself that she'd told Callie all about her parents, including their names. "What does he look like?" She had to test her somehow.

"He has hair the color of the darkest night, and the woman with him has golden hair like ye do. And there's a black horse behind him."

She still was not convinced. Everyone on and near Grant land knew what Alex and Maddie looked like and had heard of Alex's stallion, Midnight. "What else does he have to tell me?"

"Yer mother says that if ye would trust Maitland and spend yer days with him, even when he travels and leaves Grant land, ye will have a happy life. And that ye will soon need to conquer yer fears in order to save more lads and lassies from sharing yer old life, before ye were rescued. Ye must leave Grant land. But 'twill be in yer hands. Ye will have the secret he will need, though ye dinnae know it yet."

This puzzle confused her. Why would she need to leave Grant land, and how could she save anyone? Hew was long gone—he could steal away no more bairns.

"Yer father said ye need to find a place for yer square of plaid. It need no' travel with ye. Keep sewing the fold into yer skirt, but ye need no' store the square any longer. Ye are strong without it, and he is watching over ye whether ye have the square or no'."

Tears flowed down Maeve's cheeks, and she had no idea how to stop them. No one knew about the square of plaid. No one. Not even Kyla. She'd been too embarrassed to admit it to anyone. That small square gave her comfort. She hadn't started carrying it until after her father's death.

How could anyone know about it? Especially this strange, soft-spoken lass. Were her parents truly watching her from Heaven?

Baffled by this odd conversation, she wouldn't have believed a bit of it until Callie had mentioned the square of plaid. But she didn't know what to do with any of the words the lass had spoken.

"What is the secret I have?"

"I dinnae know. But I know 'tis a memory, like the memories that haunt yer dreams. Ye'll know when ye learn it, and ye'll know exactly what ye must do."

She nodded, swiping at the tears.

"Yer mother says yer true love is in the next chamber. Dinnae lose him. He will bring ye all the happiness ye long for."

She looked to the bedchamber, wondering whether to believe what she'd heard, but her mind was in too much disarray to know what to think. Secrets and plaids and love. Too much.

"Yer father said Maitland is the only one deserving of yer love."

She gasped because that was the one thing her father often said to her. One man or the other had offered for her, but his remark was always that they were not deserving of Maeve's love. Her mother had agreed. She always said, "Your true love will find you."

But he never had.

"Now yer true love has found ye. Love him

with all yer heart, Maeve." Callie smiled softly, as if she knew just how Maeve felt—confused and happy and melancholy all at the same time.

The fire popped and settled just as Maitland stepped out of the bedchamber, looking as if he was ready for bed. His feet were bare and tunic hanging loose "Come, Maeve. I will dry yer tears." Then he looked to Callie. "Do ye have any more words for us?"

"Nay, everyone who wished to speak to ye is gone. Even Mama. 'Tis time for my bed."

Maitland banked the fire, protecting the embers enough to stay warm all night. Callie retired to her own chamber.

Maeve fell into Maitland's arms and said, "Ye received a message from the heavens too?"

"Aye," he murmured, placing a soft kiss on the top of her head. "Come to bed and we can each share our experiences with the lass."

She moved into the bedchamber and vowed to do what she'd never done before.

She was about to give Maitland her heart if he wished for it.

One small tallow cast a faint light across the bedchamber. She had no idea how to handle this situation or what to do. The sweat on her palms betrayed her, but Maitland said nothing, instead clasping her hand and leading her to one side of the bed where he sat down, fitting her in beside him.

"I know not whether to believe the words the lass gave me, Maeve, but I wish to believe her words to be true."

Maeve played with the folds in her night rail, then gazed up into Maitland's warm eyes. "I received the same. Good words, words I wish to be true, but I'm unsure. What think you of Callie?"

He stared up at the small light in the chamber, pausing to gather his thoughts, but it did not take him long to answer. "I believe she is an angel sent to us. She passed words to me from Nesta, and I believe them to be true. My mother, as ye know, is a seer, a most powerful one. She believes in angels and special guidance from the heavens above. I am going to trust that Callie's words are true. What say ye?"

He waited, giving her hand a small squeeze, and she closed her eyes, a slight smile breaking out. No one knew of the plaid. No one. Callie's words to her had to have come from her dear mother and father. "I believe the same, Maitland. My sire said you would guard my heart, so if you wish, I will give it to you."

Maitland broke into a wide grin, intertwined their fingers just so, and brought his Menzie plaid from the end of the bed so a section crossed their wrists, tying them together. "Maeve, I pledge my troth and my love to ye. To honor and protect ye for as long as we both shall live. Do ye do the same with me?"

Maeve whispered, "I do. I love you, Maitland Menzie, and though I know not what life has in store for us, I trust my heart to you. Together, we will find our way, wherever it may lead."

He kissed her, pulling her close, then settled in next to her. Maeve's heart blossomed in ways she never knew existed.

CHAPTER TEN

MAITLAND AWAKENED THE next morning with a wide smile on his face. He had handfasted with Maeve, and they spent a wonderful night together. But the sun was already up, and he needed to begin his day. He wished to find food for Callie and then have her return to Grant Castle with them until the sisters returned from the abbey.

He kissed Maeve lightly on the lips so as not to awaken her, then climbed out of the cozy bed, donned his tunic, trews, and plaid, then headed to the main chamber. He picked up his hose and boots on the way, planning to put them on in the other room.

Callie was not there.

The warm home looked the same, though it was cold, so he stirred up the coals and added firewood until flames danced brightly and began to heat the small area. It was late in the day already, so he set to his tasks. He had to guess that Callie was outside taking care of her needs or looking for more firewood, but then he found a note on the table.

Surprised that Callie could write, he picked it up and scowled.

The sisters came at dawn and said we were returning to the abbey for several days. I wish ye luck on yer next travels.

He sat down in a chair with a plunk just as Maeve stepped out of the bedchamber. She blushed when she saw him, but he drew her into his arms and kissed her. "No reason to blush, Maeve. Our night together was lovely."

"Aye, it was. Where is Callie?"

He handed her the note. "Gone, it seems."

She read it quickly and looked as shocked as he felt. "She left already? The sisters were here and we never heard them?" She pulled a fur back from one of the windows and peeked outside. "Oh my goodness, half the day is gone, Maitland. We slept terribly late!"

"Aye, we did, but I enjoyed our night together, and I'm no' sorry we missed the sisters. Are ye?" He came up behind her and nuzzled her neck. "I have nice memories of our first night together. The first of many, I hope."

"I'm not sorry we missed them, but I would have liked to speak with Callie again." She paused and thought for a moment, but then she turned in his embrace and kissed him. "I too enjoyed our time together. It went by too quickly. I do not mind missing half the day. Do you?"

"I guess no'." He grabbed a pear for himself and handed one to Maeve. "This will hold us over until we can get some warm porridge in the great hall."

"If there is any left. We may have missed the midday meal too. I hope the others are not worrying about us." Shivering and covering herself with a plaid, she said, "I think I'll visit Mama's bathing chamber." Everyone knew about the chamber that Alex had built for Maddie many years ago. "If there is any hot water left."

They took care of the fire before they left, putting everything back to rights, then strolled back to the keep together. They saw no one along the way, nor any tracks in the new-fallen snow. The rain must have changed over during the night. The trees glistened with a coating of ice under the snow, and the plop-plop of melting filled the forest around them.

"Why are there no tracks?" Maitland asked.

"The sun is up and may have melted enough of the snow to obscure tracks. There isn't much snow, so it wouldn't be hard to travel. The storm was short-lived but powerful. I'll return to check on them in a fortnight or so. I would like to meet the sisters."

"Aye, the next time I'm visiting, we'll take a stroll in that direction."

As they reached the gate, a cluster of riders came into view, approaching at a swift canter. They wore the Menzie plaid.

"Maitland!" The lead rider shouted to him. Maitland recognized him as one of the senior Menzie guards.

"What is it? My mother again?"

"Nay, the lads are missing. Tad wants ye back home."

Hellfire. What else could go wrong? The lads? His stomach dropped to his knees. He fought dizziness in his head that threatened to make him heave. He must not have heard him correctly.

"The lads? Wiley and Quillan?" He caught the lead horse's bridle and held the beast still. He needed to make sure he'd heard correctly. Maeve stood right behind him.

"Aye. They disappeared last eve. We've looked everywhere, and there's no sign of them. We think the storm must have washed away any tracks, and two small boys wouldn't leave much sign of their passing to begin with."

"We'll leave as soon as I and the other men who came with me yesterday can be ready. A quarter hour, no more. Go inside for a bit to eat. Grab me a meat pie and meet me back out here. This canno' wait." He turned to Maeve. "I'm sorry, but I must go."

"Of course you must go. I wish I could do something for you."

"Ye could travel with us if ye'd like. But we will be traveling quickly. As few stops as we can."

She shook her head so quickly he knew what thought had hit her first—leaving Grant land. He understood. This was not the time to push her. Their time would come. This time was for the lads.

"Nay, I'll stay here. I'd only slow you down and be in the way. I wish you luck in finding the lads. I hope they just lost their way."

He tugged on his short beard. "Aye. Those lads are the light of my life. Two days ago, I was playing with them and teaching them how to use their slings. I'll never forgive myself if something has happened to them." His eyes misted, but he forced the tears away. Even their being lost would be dangerous. A storm like last night's could freeze a body quicker than most realized. And wolves and foxes would love a bite of a three-year-old leg. He leaned down to give her a kiss. He lingered, needing her warmth and love before he left her.

When he ended the kiss, she asked, "You will be back, will you not?"

"Maeve," he said, cupping her face. "We handfasted last eve. In my eyes, ye are my wife. Of course I will be back. I'm sorry I have to go so soon after giving ye my heart, but I hope ye understand. I must speak with Connor."

"Go along with you. I'll be fine. Do not worry on me, you have plenty on your mind."

He leaned down and whispered, "It pains me to let ye go, but I know I must." He released her, though his very soul did not wish to. He wished to spend another night with her, another day exploring the land, and another and another and another after that. But it was not to be. Yet.

He was halfway to the keep when Connor came flying out the door. "'Tis true? Tad's laddies are missing?"

"Aye. I know no' much about it, but could I ask for yer assistance? Mayhap a score of guards to help us with the search? I dinnae believe the English are behind it—we've sent them running, and they'll not be back until after the snows. And reivers have been scarce, too. I dinnae know what's happening, but there's something odd going on."

The door opened behind Connor, and Alasdair joined them. "I heard. I'll go with ye."

Connor nodded. "Alasdair, choose two score men to travel with us. I'd like ye to lead the guards."

"Possible battle or just search patrol?" Alasdair asked as Dyna came up behind him.

"We dinnae know," Maitland replied. "Dyna will tell ye the English we've met up with have been much different than any others we've met. No careful lines to fight, no uniforms. They act like the Borderland reivers of old times. I dinnae think they would be after bairns, but we dinnae know for sure. The lads could have just gotten caught in the storm, or perchance someone took them for some unknown reason. We Menzies are a strong clan, but we've no treasures to pay in ransom."

"It could be the English," Dyna said. "We killed some, but some survived and headed south. Could this be a last foray of retaliation before the snows?"

Maitland shook his head. "'Tis certainly within the realm of possibility, though my gut says no'. The English are bastards, no doubt, but soldiers have no use for bairns."

"I'm coming with ye, Maitland. I'll not leave ye to do this alone. We work well together. Derric will be fine with all the help he has here. I'll get the horses ready for travel." Dyna clapped his shoulder as she moved past him toward the gates.

"My thanks, Dyna. I'll no' reject any help." Maitland went inside and grabbed half a loaf of bread and spoke to his men, who were eating porridge. "As soon as ye are finished, we'll be on our way. Grab food to eat on the way. We'll no' be stopping."

He hurried to his chamber and grabbed the pack he'd arrived with just the day before. He hated to leave Maeve, but he had no choice. They'd made their vows, and he intended to keep them. He needed to make sure her chieftain— and brother—knew of their promises to each other. He found Jamie out near the stables.

"Jamie, a word before I go, if ye please."

Jamie nodded. "I heard of yer troubles. We'll help in any way we can." He followed Maitland out to a spot away from the group assembling to leave.

Maitland took a deep breath and made his confession. "Maeve and I handfasted last eve. I would have asked yer permission, but it happened without warning. I hope ye will still approve and bless our union. Circumstances that we hadn't expected came up, and we made the decision mutually. I'm in love with yer sister, and I saw no reason to wait. We are old enough to know our own minds and hearts."

Jamie clasped his shoulder. "Welcome to Clan Grant, Menzie. I approve and am very happy for Maeve and ye. The whole clan will rejoice at the news. I hope ye can eventually convince her to travel to Menzie land with ye."

"Aye, I share that hope. Many thanks to ye."

Maitland found Maeve readying his horse. He swept her into his arms and said, "I just told yer brother I'm in love with ye and that we handfasted. I hope ye approve. He gave us his approval." Then he kissed her, a passionate kiss to let her know that she would indeed be missed.

"Godspeed," she whispered. "Find those boys, Maitland. And then return to me as soon as you can. I'm in love with you too."

The combined Menzie and Grant forces thundered along the road a moment later. Their numbers neared three score with the two groups of Menzie guards and two score Grant guards.

Maitland talked strategies with Alasdair, Dyna, and Connor along the way, but they came up with no solid reasoning for a possible kidnapping. The trip was torturously long, but it gave him time to think on all that had happened. A sound mind helped to build a strong plan of attack.

They weren't far from Menzie land when they met a patrol led by Maitland's brother Tomag.

"Greetings, Connor." Tomag pulled up so they could speak. "Our thanks for bringing extra men. Grant guards are always welcome aid."

"Ye would do no less for us."

"Have the patrols turned up anything yet, Tomag?" Maitland asked. "Do ye know anything at all about where they are?" He was anxious to form a plan, see what they'd already tried.

Tomag sighed and motioned for them to move away from the main path. "We have," he said quietly. "Tad had a messenger last night. The lads are fine but they are hidden away. They will return them on one condition."

Maitland was taken aback by this news. "A kidnapping for ransom? What the hell could they want? We'll pay them whatever coin they wish."

"Not coin," Tomag said.

"Then what?"

"They want Ada."

"Ada?" Connor asked. "Why would they want Tad's wife?"

Maitland's heart nearly ripped apart. His stomach dropped to his toes, and he came close to heaving in the bushes. But rage overwhelmed his initial sick reaction. A fire began to burn deep in his belly, the need for revenge.

"I know why."

The other men and Dyna all turned to stare at him. Tomag asked, "Why? What could they possibly want with a woman who's carrying? Not for marriage or as a whore."

The memory of Callie's words ripped through him. That Nesta said they'd locked the two of them in the dungeon not because of anything he'd done, and not for any kind of information. They wanted their child.

Maitland's words came out in a whisper. "They want the bairn. Just like they wanted our bairn from Nesta. To sell. Some people will do anything for a newborn bairn to raise as their own."

CHAPTER ELEVEN

MAEVE WATCHED THEM go, her heart
sick. Just last night, she'd married this
man, who she'd fallen in love with against all
her expectations, and now he was leaving her.

He wasn't leaving *her*. He had to go, for Wiley
and Quillan. She had no doubt in her mind about
that, but she should have gone with him.

But she couldn't.

Jamie came up and wrapped an arm around
her shoulders. "He shall return for ye, Maeve.
Congratulations to ye both. I believe ye will be
verra happy together."

She turned to her brother, eyes filled with tears.
"Why can I not leave Grant land? I have to learn.
I wish to be able to go with him wherever life
takes me. I should have gone with him now, but
I couldn't. I just…"

"Nay," Jamie said, turning her around and
leading her back into the keep. "Nay, they will
be traveling too fast for ye, Maeve. And he needs
to be able to focus on the lads. Ye would be a
distraction for him at this point. Come, let's find
Kyla and ye can give her the happy news. We will

have a celebration when he's back with ye. Think on that—his return."

Jamie took her to the tower room where Kyla's family spent most of their time. Kyla, Gracie, and Emmalin, Alasdair's wife, sat together in front of the fire.

"Ladies," Jamie said, squeezing Maeve's shoulders, "Maeve has some news for ye. I'll be taking my leave but thought ye could help settle her. As ye probably heard, Maitland left because his two young nephews are missing."

"Maeve, come join us," Gracie said. "The news from Clan Menzie upsets me. I always worry that could happen to any of our wee ones someday. But tell us yer news first. I hope 'tis good news."

Jamie waved to his wife as he left the group, closing the door behind him quietly.

Maeve glanced around the group, not sure where to start. Before any words could come, she burst into tears.

Kyla hurried over and led her to a chair. "Maeve, what is it?"

She let out a sob and said, "Maitland and I handfasted last eve and…"

Kyla giggled and said, "That is the best news I have heard in a long while. Why are ye crying about it?"

Gracie said, "Maeve, 'tis wonderful. Ye will make a great pair!"

"Congratulations!" Emmalin smiled and reached over to squeeze Maeve's hand. "'Tis too much emotion for ye, perhaps?"

"I feel like I just lost my husband. I waited so

long, and I do love him, but he left and he had
to so I cannot blame him. I wanted him to go
and I'm too scared to go with him and what if
he hates me for it and how will I ever be able
to leave because I have to go meet his family
because he had two brothers and a sister and two
nephews and oh, what do I do?"

The three women all giggled and jumped
up and joined together to wrap her in a single
embrace.

When they finally took their seats again and
Maeve stopped her tears, she giggled, so grateful
for her large family. "My thanks to you for making
me laugh about it."

Kyla said, "Maeve, ye have a large heart. Papa
always said ye did. He would be so happy for ye.
And Maitland will return. He is an honorable
man. And we can all tell he's smitten with ye."

"And braw too," Emmalin whispered.

Gracie nodded her agreement. "And once this
episode is ended and ye have time to get used to
each other, I believe ye will be able to travel with
him. Mayhap one of us will go with ye if that
will make ye more comfortable. But we all know
he will keep ye safe. I think ye will learn to love
traveling."

Emmalin said, "Marriage is scary at first, but
ye'll get more comfortable with him. My guess is
that if ye handfasted last eve ye dinnae sleep much.
Are ye overtired mayhap?" Then she waggled her
brow at Maeve, and the group broke into giggles
again.

Once the laughter settled down and her face

cooled, Maeve said, "You are all correct. And the truth is I am exhausted. I think I will take a wee nap. My thanks for your support. I do not know what I would do without you, sisters."

She got up to leave but then paused. "By the way, Maitland and I met a lass named Callie who just moved into a hut in the forest with three nuns who took her in after her mama died. Know you anything about her? We sheltered with her during the storm but when we awakened, she was gone. It was the oddest thing…"

Gracie looked at Kyla, both shaking their heads. Gracie finally said, "I have no knowledge of anyone living there, but I'll have Jamie check."

"No need to bother. They left on a short trip but said they'll be back in a sennight or so. I'll check myself when they return."

She climbed the stairs to her bedchamber, thinking on all that had been said. Maitland would return, she was certain of that. The only question was, would her nightmares return too?

And what would he think of them?

"Ye are no' going anywhere, Ada." Tad paced the hall and stared at his wife. "How can ye think to give in to their demands?"

She rubbed her protruding belly as they discussed the situation in the great hall. Tears flowed freely down her cheeks. "Because I want my laddies back. Tad, I could no' bear to lose them. What will we do?" She flipped her blonde plait over her shoulder.

Maitland saw the sheen of unfallen tears in Tad's eyes, too. If it were his lads taken, his Maeve in danger, he wasn't sure he could keep from weeping. He had to help his brother with this.

They had to find the lads.

"I have reason to believe that the men who kidnapped Nesta and me were after our child instead of us."

"Maitland, ye've never mentioned this. Why now all of a sudden?" his father asked.

He didn't know how to explain it with so many listening so he dodged the question, with a wee bit of truth in it. "Take it as kind of a dream. I'm no' certain, but 'tis entirely possible that was what the men wanted with Nesta. And I've been thinking on what happened that day and the different incidents we've had of men taking bairns and children to sell. The facts match. 'Tis all I'll say for now."

Connor stroked his chin. "'Tis good to have an idea of the bastards' plan, but unless ye can lead us directly to where ye were held, Maitland, it will no' help us find them faster, I'm sorry to say. As far as I recall, ye have no memory of where ye were held, correct?"

"Aye, I dinnae know. They beat me and left me in the forest. Tad found me." How he wished he could offer more information. All he knew was that it had taken hours to return to their castle from where he was found.

Connor turned to Tad. "What is yer timeline? When do ye have to take Ada to them?"

"This eve at dusk. We're to meet at the fork in

the main road to the north. They say they'll trade the lads for Ada."

"Ye should no' believe them. If they are taking bairns to sell, they'll want to keep the lads, too. I have a suggestion," Maitland said, glancing over at Dyna, who nodded her agreement.

"Go ahead," Tad said. "I'm looking for solutions."

"We send out patrols in groups of six men, looking for anything unusual. They need to check any abandoned dwellings, look for anyone to question. We search for any unusual activity."

"We've already started that with no results. We only have a couple of hours, Maitland. Our best bet is to give them Ada, and then we can attack after they leave. Grab Ada after we have the lads in our clutches." Tad paced back and forth as he spoke, tugging on his hair. "But I refuse to give them Ada."

"Tad, I can get away. They'll no' give us the lads unless I go willingly. We have no choice." She continued to rub her belly.

"Oh, I think we do," Maitland said. He grinned and tipped his head toward Dyna.

She stepped into the middle of the group with a pillow held to her front and said, "Wrap me up, Da. I just became several months pregnant. Make it a Menzie plaid and I'm ready to go."

Connor and Maitland both grinned. Connor said, "'Tis yer best bet. Dyna is also a seer, and if there's trouble, she may be able to see it coming."

Maitland grabbed two Menzie plaids, handed one to Connor and the two worked until they had Dyna looking the same exact size as Ada. They gave her a shawl to put over her head to shield her face, to further confuse the kidnappers.

Dyna stood next to Ada with a wide grin and said, "I'm ready!"

"Let's go," Maitland said.

They had to get their boys back, and they could not make any mistakes.

CHAPTER TWELVE

SOMEWHERE IN A cellar in a small castle in the woods...

"I don yike it here, Wi," Q said. "I wanna doe home."

"Hush, Q, we will soon. Ye know Papa will find us." The two were in a small chamber with a funny-looking door on it. There was no door handle and there was a window at the top to peek through, but they were too short to see out. They had one pallet and one blanket to share.

"But Papa be mad at us."

"We only went outside the curtain wall because we heard the puppies. We didnae know they were bad men. They'll still come for us."

"How dey find us?"

"Papa and our uncles are the smartest ever. They'll find us."

"Papa and uncas will come soon? 'Tis dirty here. An I'm tode."

"Use the blanket, Q. I dinnae need it. We have to think of something."

"Why?"

"Because. What if Papa comes and he only

looks abovestairs? He'll no' know where we are. But we can fix it."

"How we fixit?"

"We are in the cellar. I dinnae wish to be in the cellar. Papa could come and knock on the door and he'll no' know we are here. If we were outside, we could hide in the trees until Papa comes."

"Can we doe ouside?"

A voice on the other side of the door said, "Ye lads be quiet. Don't be planning something foolish, or ye won't get any food."

"Give us food. We hungwy," Q called.

"Shut yer mouth. Ye'll get yer food when the sun sets, and not before."

Then they heard the man walk down the passageway.

"Q, do ye have yer sling and yer sack?"

"Aye, in my fode." He patted the side of his plaid where their mother had sewn a fold to let them tuck small things away.

"Have ye any stones?"

He shook his head.

"We need to find some. Let's look in the corners." The two moved to different areas of the chamber, eyes on the floor.

"I foun one," Q said. "And I haf two." He held them up to show his brother.

"Good. Put them in yer sack. Keep looking."

They searched the corners, under a bowl in one spot, and then an idea came to Wiley. "Under the pallet! Let's look there."

They lifted the small mattress together. To their

delight, a scattering of small stones covered the floor. More than they could fit in their sack. Q looked at him wide-eyed and smiled.

"We have dem. What we do?"

"First, we'll put a bunch on the floor near the door so when someone walks inside, he'll step on them. Remember Loki's story about putting the stones in the man's shoes? If he steps on a bunch of them, it will hurt and he'll look at his feet. Then we'll launch stones at his face with our slings."

"Dey are pig-nuts. Piggy nuts." He grinned at his own jest.

"Ye mean surly pig-nuts. 'Tis Loki's name for them."

The two set to work, and when they were satisfied with their layer of stones, pointy sides up whenever possible, they sat side by side on the pallet and waited.

"I'm hungwy and tode," Q said. "I wan Papa."

"Dinnae worry, Q. Mama will give us all the fruit tarts ye wish for once they find us."

He smiled and said, "Pwomise?"

"Hush. Someone is coming."

CHAPTER THIRTEEN

MAEVE BOLTED UP in her bed. She'd just had a horrible nightmare, but she had to forget her terror and find Maisie. This time, the nightmare had been more than darkness.

She knew where the lads were.

She hurried down the passageway, down the stairs and toward Maisie's tower, but then stopped. Maisie stood in front of the hearth as if she were waiting for her.

"You had a dream?" Maeve asked. It was odd how often their nightmares came in the same form on the same nights.

"Aye. Did you?"

"Aye. I know where the lads are being held." Maeve shivered, a sudden understanding coursing through her. Callie's words about having the secret came back to Maeve. Was this it?

"I think I do too. Tell me about your dream." Maisie sat in the closest chair.

"I was standing in the doorway to a chamber, listening to two men talk."

Maisie nodded, tears making her eyes glisten. "Go on."

"One said to the other that the reason he'd stolen all the lassies is because you could make good coin selling bairns. Especially the younger ones. But he said infants are too much trouble, so he had them stolen between the ages of one and five. He said he stole me away from a cottage next to yours. There was only a mother, no father, so he killed her and stole me away. He said that if anything happened to him, the other man was to sell the bairns."

"I saw the same thing."

"Who were they? If I knew who they were, I could tell Maitland." Maeve shivered, moving closer to the dying embers in the hearth. "They could be the ones holding the laddies."

"I know them. It was Hew. It took me a while to work out who the other man was. It was Hew's son. I remembered when he called Hew 'Da.'"

"Aye, I heard him call him his father. Oh, Maisie, do you think this could be the solution?" Maeve's hope blossomed deep inside her.

"Aye. The younger one said he would follow the plan and keep selling bairns, and he got away when Hew was killed."

"We have to tell Maitland." If she only knew how they could tell him. They could find him, but she wished to be the one to tell him. Her mind shied away from the implications of this entire situation.

Gracie came into the hall and hurried over to them, wrapping her night rail around her. "What's happening? Why are ye both out here in the middle of the night?"

"We know who kidnapped the lads. We both had the same dream," Maeve explained, rubbing her eyes.

"Truly? The same exact dream? Who did it?"

"Hew Gordon's son. He promised his father he would continue to sell bairns. It was to be his sire's legacy. His name is…" Maeve paused and looked to Maisie for help, shaking her head because she couldn't quite catch the name in her memory.

"Hugo!" Maisie blurted out.

"That's right!"

Gracie said, "I'm going to get Jamie and Alaric. Alaric will go and tell Maitland what ye've discovered."

"Nay," Maeve said, grabbing Gracie's hand. "I wish to go with him."

Gracie arched her brow at Maeve. "Are ye certain, Maeve? If it were me, I would go, but ye havenae traveled much."

"Nay. I need to do this. Will he know where to find Hugo?"

"Nay, probably not."

Jamie came out behind his wife, wrapping his plaid around him. "I overheard. Maitland willnae, but Alasdair will. Jake showed him where Hew Gordon lived, in case there were ever any more problems. It's between here and Menzie land, I believe, but hidden and hard to find."

"I must get dressed," Maeve said.

Gracie followed her. "Maeve, I'll pack for ye. When was the last time ye packed to travel? Know ye what to take in a saddlebag?"

Maeve chuckled. "Nay. I welcome your assistance. I would not know where to start."

Maeve was leaving Grant land.

The fork in the road where they were to meet the kidnappers was quiet, as if the forest around them waited for the conflict to come.

Maitland stood with Dyna next to him, all chubby and cute. He could not stand the silence any longer. "Wish I'd seen ye when ye carried yer bairns."

"I was bonny. Was I no', Papa?"

"All three times. Bonny and big as a…"

"Watch it…"

Connor chuckled but didn't add anything. "I think someone is coming."

"I see them too."

Maitland blew out a quiet breath. "'Tis a good thing my brother didnae come with us or he would be bolting out there now. And I understand. I'm having a hard time not doing the same. I dinnae see any lads with them." Both groups remained on horseback.

"Nay," Alasdair whispered. "Seven men I count. Mayhap eight."

They waited for the men to approach them, their horses surrounding Dyna's horse as if she were the most precious of all. They'd made sure the cushion under Dyna's plaid looked as much like the belly of a woman carrying a child as possible. Her hair color was almost the same as Ada's, though a shade or two lighter because

Dyna's was nearly white. But close enough. They just had to hope the kidnappers weren't familiar enough with Ada to see the difference.

"Remember," Connor said. "Ye must hold yer tempers if this becomes a fight. Kill them all, and we'll have no idea where the lads are." They'd brought two more guards, the number they'd been allowed to bring. Five total.

Of course, there was another score hiding in the trees, waiting to attack at the sound of a war whoop or bird whistle, but they were well-trained and would not reveal themselves until time.

The kidnappers were almost upon them when Maitland bellowed, "Where are the lads?"

The man in the center said, "Send over the lass and we'll tell ye where to find them."

"Nay," Maitland said. "Tell us where the lads are first."

They came with eight men against their five, but Dyna was worth two. She had her bow well hidden.

"They're lying," Dyna said. "They'll no' tell ye anything. Let me go back with them."

Connor said, "That willnae happen, Dyna."

"Let them take me."

Maitland whispered, "Nay, Dyna. Ye can read them as well as I. They are about to attack, I can see it in their eyes. They think they can kill us, take ye, and then run."

Alasdair said, "My insides are laughing hysterically, I just want ye to know. I wish to see any one of them try to take Dyna."

"Leave one alive," Maitland reminded them.

A whistle came from the opposing group, and they pulled out their small swords and came straight for them, a direct attack. Maitland had known it was about to happen, but they hadn't counted on the ten more men on horseback coming out of the woods to join the eight.

Alasdair's war whoop brought the rest of the Grant and Menzie men out of the woods, and the battle was on.

Maitland warned, "Dinnae go with them, Dyna."

Dyna stayed calm until someone tried to grab her and she could no longer play the quiet lass. If Maitland wasn't fighting for his own life, he would have smiled. Out came her dagger and she slashed the man's sword arm. His sword fell uselessly to the ground. Then she pulled out her bow and nocked an arrow, spinning to look for a clear shot. Any time a man made her his target, he fell with an arrow in his chest.

The Grants and Menzies cut the enemy down in short order, making sure to wound and not kill several of them so they could question them. A few of their own men took minor wounds, but even that much made them upset. Their two clans rarely lost a fight.

The skirmish ended and Maitland felt no better for it. He motioned to Connor and Alasdair and said, "Have the men find some to question. Hold them separately, and we can compare their answers."

"Please. Allow me," Dyna said. "I'd like to hear how they justify stealing bairns."

"Nay, ye are too emotionally involved because they're bairns," Alasdair said. "I know ye. Stay up there on yer horse and watch for others coming out of the woods."

Dyna snarled, but Alasdair was right. Dyna's temper always flared when the safety of children was involved.

"Punching bollocks doesnae work, Dyna. They cannae speak then," Maitland drawled. The other men laughed and winced at the same time.

He dismounted, and with Connor and Alasdair, questioned any man who could speak, but they were greatly disappointed. None of the men knew who had hired them, and they all claimed to know nothing about the location of the two lads.

The last one said, "They offered us coin to fight in one skirmish. All we had to do was attack and grab the woman. That was all. We never heard anything about any lads."

"Where did ye meet with him? Were ye in a castle, a hut, a manor home? Where?"

"Three men came to the Borderlands and hired us. Said we'd be home within two days. They fed us and spoke about the head man but never named him proper. I heard one of them mention his first name."

"Which is?"

"Hugo. 'Tis all we know. They called him Hugo. Nothing else to tell ye."

"Watch over them. I have to think." Maitland took his horse and headed back out to the main path, Alasdair, Connor, and Dyna going with him.

"I think they're being truthful," Connor said. "We are no further ahead except for the name Hugo. That mean anything to ye, Menzie?"

Maitland shook his head. "I believe them too. But that tells us naught. Whoever these bastards are, they're being careful to hide their tracks."

"I think we have to step up the patrols," Alasdair said. "Search every building. We've got enough men to canvas a good area."

The sound of approaching horses caught their ears, so they backed off the path and waited. Maitland said, "Better no' be another ambush."

Dyna moved next to him. "'Tis a main path. Likely to be usual travelers. Try to take yer emotions out of this, Maitland. It's hard, but ye must try. Ye can think better if yer mind is clear."

He did his best to do that but he was devastated that this had been a failure. Where the hell were the lads? If he went back to Menzie Castle without them, his brother would go mad. He did his best to focus, looking to see who was approaching, but what he saw nearly undid him.

Maeve was coming straight toward him.

CHAPTER FOURTEEN

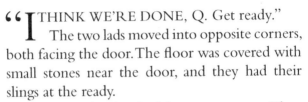

"ITHINK WE'RE DONE, Q. Get ready."
The two lads moved into opposite corners, both facing the door. The floor was covered with small stones near the door, and they had their slings at the ready.

They waited and waited, but no one came. Then footsteps sounded as if someone was coming toward them, then whoever it was turned back and went the other way.

"Q, can ye cry or something? Make them come this way. Tell them ye are sick."

"Aye." He let out a wail and called, "I hungwy! I sick. Pweez bring somping to eat." Then he let out some real tears, and Wiley feared he wouldn't be able to use his sling.

"Good work, Q! That must bring someone. Now be strong for Mama and Papa. Uncle Maitland said we have to be strong."

Quillan brushed away the tears and stared at the door wide-eyed. Wiley took a deep breath and tried to ignore his own hunger and fear. He could be brave, too.

Someone outside their door coughed, and

this time the footsteps kept coming. "Shut up. Ye better not be sick. If ye heave, ye'll have to clean it up. Not me. I'm bringing ye some bread!" Then the man laughed. "Let's see if ye can catch it when I toss it at ye." He came to the window and threw a piece of bread in but it didn't reach them, landing on the floor directly in front of the window.

Q let out a loud wail. The man cursed and took a key and put it in the lock, muttering. "Damn lads." Then he opened the door and stepped inside, his feet hitting the stones. He lost his balance and teetered.

"Now, Q!" Wiley shouted.

The two peppered his face with stones, and he cursed and raised his arms, trying to stop the stones from hitting him. "I'll kill ye lads. Wait until I get ye. I'll beat both yer behinds."

"Nay ye willnae. We are Menzies. Run, Q!"

The two ran right by him, slingers still gripped tight in their hands. "Ye are mean," Wiley said when he passed him. "And ugly."

"I don yike ye." Q stopped to kick their guard in the leg from behind, but a hand swung around and grabbed him.

"Ye wee brat. I'll fix ye." The man had a tight grip on Q's arm.

"Hep! Hep me, Wi!"

Wiley's next stone from his sling hit the brute square in the eye. He howled and let go of Q.

"I'll kill ye both!"

The brothers barreled down the passageway. "Run, Q!"

"I wunnin," he said, from right behind his brother. They raced up the stairs and saw a door at the top. Wiley pushed at it, reaching for the door handle, barely able to reach it. "I canno' reach it, Q. What do we do?"

The man started up the steps toward them, but Wiley and Q launched the last of their stones. The man slipped and fell backwards down the stairs, landing flat on his back. He moaned and raised his head, then lay still.

"We have to get out the door, Q. Help me find something to stand on." He looked around for something to step on but saw nothing. "Do ye think ye could work the latch if ye could reach it?"

"Yike wen we took the honey cakes off da table?"

"Aye, like that." He got down on all fours, crouching low so the smaller boy could get onto his back, then slowly straightened his arms. With this boost, Q could reach the latch. The door swung open a wee bit.

"I dot it!" Q cheered.

Wiley scrambled to his feet, and the two headed out the door.

Then Wiley stopped and reached back to take his brother's hand.

He heard a war whoop and thundering hooves. What was going on?

CHAPTER FIFTEEN

MAITLAND WAS SO pleased to see his wife coming toward him that he nearly yelled, but then fear shot into him. Had something else happened? He urged his horse into a gallop toward the group. Alaric and Alick rode on either side of Maeve.

"What happened? Why are ye here, Maeve? Are ye hale?" His throat had a lump in it. He couldn't move. First his mother, then the lads, now his wife? He could only take so much.

"Nay, naught is wrong," Alaric said. "We think she knows where the lads are."

Connor joined them. "If ye have any ideas, Maeve, tell us."

Maeve looked directly at Alasdair and said, "Maisie and I had the same dream last night, and she recognized the men in it—Hew and his son Hugo. Hew is dead, but Hugo still lives. We think he's holding the lads in his castle, but we couldn't tell what castle it was."

"Da thinks ye know where it is, Alasdair," Alaric said. "He thought Uncle Jake took ye there once to show ye where it is."

Alasdair closed his eyes and thought for a moment. "He did. I'll never forget it in all my days. Castle Dubh."

Maeve began to sob. Maitland moved next to her, then leaned over and scooped her up to set her in his saddle in front of him. He wrapped his arms around her from behind her and said, "Well done, love. We'll find them now."

"Can ye take us there? How far away from here?" Connor asked.

"About an hour's ride from here. 'Tis no' a large castle but 'tis verra well hidden. I will make one request to all."

They all nodded. They knew what he was asking.

"The right is yers, Alasdair," Maitland said. "If we find the lads, I'll gladly give ye that right." He knew the man wished to avenge the wrong done his mother, Aline, so many years ago.

And probably Maeve, Morna, and Maisie too. But he wouldn't do that to Maeve right now. She didn't need to worry about him. He'd find the lads and come home so they could start their life as husband and wife.

"Maeve, I have to send ye to Menzie Castle. Will ye wait for me there? My mother will be happy to meet ye."

"We'll escort her," Alick said.

"My thanks. Ye and yer men should stay the night. I'm hoping we'll be having a large celebration in a couple of hours."

The groups separated, and Alasdair took the lead. "I dinnae recall much about the castle, but they do have dungeons in the cellars, so be aware that the lads could be hidden there. The castle is positioned partway up a small hill, and it is no' easy to see. Blends in with the rocks around it."

"Curtain wall? Moat?" Connor asked.

"Only a crumbling curtain wall is my recollection. Ye can walk right up to the keep. It had three doors, one on the side, plus the front and back."

The group that rode out was now three score, with the addition of a few who joined them from Alick's group. It took about another hour plus a half of slow progress through the forest before Alasdair motioned for them to be quiet. He and Dyna scouted ahead, where Maitland could see a rocky gray rise beyond the trees, then returned to the others to plan their attack.

Dyna explained what they discovered, "There is a small group in the back where they're roasting a boar. It looks like the leader is there based on the quality of his clothing. He'll be easy for Alasdair to take out. Otherwise there is a group of ten men on the side, all deep in their cups. No visible lads, so my guess is they are being held inside."

Alasdair nodded agreement. "Maitland, the men are to the right of the keep and around back. There's a side door for ye to take on the left. Ye'll want to go yerself to fetch the lads, I'm guessing. That side door will be yer way inside while we go around to the right. Who are ye taking with ye?"

Dyna blurted, "Me! I'm going with him."

Maitland nodded. "The two of us will find

them." He felt confident. Everything he'd learned over the last day or two was falling into place. Maeve, Nesta, Callie. Things had taken a wild turn, but a good one. The lads would be home safe in no time, and he was finally getting answers to his many questions.

They advanced quietly, some dismounting, others forming a line of mounted warriors.

Maitland and Dyna moved forward together and found the side door just where Alasdair said it would be. They waited a distance away and listened for the attack to start—most of it would be out of their sight—and they wanted anyone inside to rush out to join the castle's defense before they went in.

The door swung open, and Maitland drew his sword. But to his surprise, two laddies crept out and froze.

Wiley and Q. They stared for a moment, then Alasdair's war whoop broke the tableau.

The two lads raced forward.

"Papa, where are ye?" Then their eyes fell on him. "Uncle Maitland!"

Maitland dropped his sword and hurried up the hill, needing to get the lads under cover just in case the battle spread to this side of the castle. Dyna caught his lead and waited, an arrow on her bowstring, in case someone came around to stop them. The boys barreled down the hill at a dead run, Wiley so fast that Q, lagging behind but refusing to let go of his brother's hand, fell twice, forcing Wiley to stop and help him back up. Maitland held his arms out, the tears flowing down his cheeks, and the two ran into them, squealing and talking all at once. He scooped them up, one under each arm, and dashed for the cover of the forest, where Dyna waited.

Q stepped back and said, "Why ye cwy, Unca?"

"Because I missed ye. Boys cry too."

"Ye are crying and so is Dyna," Wiley said. "See, I told ye they would come for us, Q."

Dyna gave them each a hug.

Wiley laughed, that contagious laugh he always had. He'd never been so happy to see two people in his life. "Uncle Maitland, we got him with our slings and put stones on the floor and Q kicked him when we ran away..."

The side door opened again, and they stopped to see who it was.

"Lads, come back here!" An old man stood outside the door, looking around for his missing captives. Then he noticed the horses and heard the melee. He seemed to forget the lads and ran toward the back of the castle.

The boys hid behind Maitland, watching the man as if he were a hornet who might sting at any moment. "I've got ye, lads. He'll no' bother ye again. Let's go back to the horses."

"Unca Mawin, I'm hungwy."

"I think I have something for ye."

By the time they got back to where they'd left their horses tethered, the rest of the group was already returning. They looked as though they'd been out for a pleasant ride, no more.

Alasdair came first. He came right over to Maitland and tousled the hair on both boys' heads, smiling despite his watery eyes. "Well done, Maitland."

"Yer parents are avenged?"

Alasdair nodded. "They are. And Maeve, Morna, and Maisie and anyone else they harmed."

"Where's Papa?" Wiley asked.

"He stayed home to protect yer mother. We'll go straight there now."

"Unca Mawin, I ride wif ye?"

"Aye, Q. Wiley, which horse would ye like to ride on?"

He pointed to Alasdair's towering black warhorse. "Can I ride that one? Or with Dyna?"

Dyna came over and patted Midnight's nose, the only horse allowed to carry the single name of Midnight in honor of its sire. "This horse is even more special than mine. Alasdair, what do ye think? Can he hold both of ye?"

The horse whinnied and tossed its mane. "Can I pet him?" Wiley asked.

"Here's an apple. Give him this. He'll be gentle. He loves apples."

Wiley held the treat out and the beast tipped his head down, smelled the apple, then took it gently while both boys giggled.

Maitland breathed a deep sigh of relief and happiness. He glanced up at the castle, grateful his nephews were no longer trapped inside it. What kind of evil person would steal bairns to sell? A new chill ran through him quickly.

"Dyna, watch the lads for a moment? I need to check something."

"Of course."

"I'll be right back, lads. I wish to make sure the castle is empty and there's no one left to bother us again." This was a good enough reason for the boys. He had to check something for himself.

He strode across the yard and into the side door, down the steps, and into the cellar. He stopped to take everything in. There was storage to one side, a buttery and other rooms, but he didn't care so much about that. It was the other passage that drew him.

He found a lit torch and took it off the wall, carrying it with him down the corridor. There were four cells, all empty. He had to smile when he passed the second one, because he knew it had housed the lads. There were stones everywhere, especially by the door. How proud he was of both of them!

Moving to the one on the end, he stopped and looked through the barred window to see if it looked familiar. It did. It had been his.

New tears flowed down his cheeks as he relived that awful night in his life. He had no memory of the outside of the castle or the cellar because he'd shut down once he'd held Nesta's lifeless body in his arms.

He moved to the cell next to it. This was it. Nesta delivered their bairn and then died in that cell in front of him. He contained his sobs, swiped the wetness from his cheek. "I love ye, Nesta, but I love Maeve too. I'll no' forget ye."

Callie had been right. Everything she'd told them had been true.

He headed back out the door and heard the

best sound ever. "Unca Mawin! We doein home now?"

"Aye, Q. We're going home."

Dyna asked, "Ye find what ye needed to find?"

"Aye. This was the place." He shook his head, still shocked. "All this time I'd thought we'd been taken by the English. But it had been Scots who held us captive."

Wiley looked at him and asked, "Are ye crying again?"

"Aye, but from happiness. I canno' wait to go home to see yer mama and papa. They will be so glad to see ye, lads." He reached into his saddlebag and said, "Here. I have some dried meat for ye both to chew on." He gave them each a share, then said, "Are ye ready, Wiley? Are ye ready to climb onto Midnight?"

Wiley nodded.

Alasdair mounted and said, "Come on up. Ye can pet him from up here while he chews on another apple."

"He has big teeth." Wiley squealed when Dyna boosted him up onto the massive black warhorse and set him in front of Alasdair. Then Maitland mounted, and Dyna helped the smaller boy onto his saddle. Both horses got their apples.

Q turned around and asked, "We doe see Mama and Papa now?"

"Aye, we go see Mama and Papa now, wee warrior. Here's a piece of cheese for ye."

Maitland wished to hold him tight all the way home, but he contained himself.

The tears? Those he couldn't contain.

CHAPTER SIXTEEN

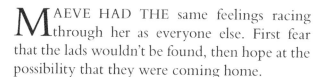

MAEVE HAD THE same feelings racing through her as everyone else. First fear that the lads wouldn't be found, then hope at the possibility that they were coming home.

Tomag had been waiting at the edge of Menzie land with his father and a few other guards, ready to escort the warriors back.

She'd been welcomed with open arms by Avelina and Drew, both pleased to hear they'd handfasted.

"As good as married in my eyes and God's," Drew had said. "We welcome ye to Clan Menzie, Maeve. Our son is a wee bit stubborn at times, but 'tis much there to love too."

She'd agreed wholeheartedly.

As she stood at the top of the parapets next to Avelina and Ada, forever hopeful they would see two wee lads on horseback, the Menzie war whoop floated over the landscape before she had even caught sight of a single rider. Cheers rose from every corner of Menzie land at the sound.

It was Maitland's voice that set her to crying. As soon as she caught sight of the wee laddie on Maitland's lap, she crumpled against the wall, sobbing over all the pain one horrid man and his legacy had caused. She thought of how her mother had been murdered, with herself so young she didn't even have a memory of her to hold on to, of Maisie and Morna and Aline, about how Callie had said Maitland's wife had died from losing their child and how they could have been kidnapped for the same reason. It all fell together into a path of evil scheming, of deceit and cruelty unlike she'd ever imagined.

How she prayed that legacy had finally come to an end.

The others had already headed down the stairs when the wee voices of two lads carried to her. "Mama! Papa! We're home! Look at me on the big warhorse! He likes me too."

"Mama, can I haf a fwuit tart?"

Maeve rushed down the stairs to greet the wee returning heroes. And Maitland and the other men, as well.

Before she knew it, two arms wrapped around her waist and pulled her tight, the scent of her dear husband telling her who it was. She sobbed and sobbed as if finally able to rid her body of the nightmare that had gripped her for so many years. So sure that it had finally ended she pulled a small piece of plaid out of her skirt fold, kissed it, and let it fly into the air.

She was leaving the past behind her and vowed to embrace this new life.

EPILOGUE

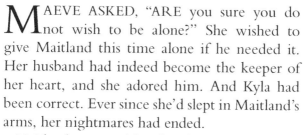

MAEVE ASKED, "ARE you sure you do not wish to be alone?" She wished to give Maitland this time alone if he needed it. Her husband had indeed become the keeper of her heart, and she adored him. And Kyla had been correct. Ever since she'd slept in Maitland's arms, her nightmares had ended.

Maitland squeezed her hand. "I've been alone long enough in my life."

He'd made a makeshift grave for Nesta, a place where he could honor her memory even though there were no bones to bury. Many times over the years he'd tried to do the same, but he just couldn't do it. Now was the right time. He'd carved a beautiful wooden cross for her grave marker so she'd be represented in the Clan Menzie cemetery. He knelt down and placed it just right, then placed a bouquet of red berries, pinecones, and holly in front of the cross. His mother had made it in Nesta's memory.

He said a quick prayer and was about to leave when an odd vision appeared in front of them. A quivering visage became a beautiful red-haired woman in a flowing white gown.

"Are those angel wings?" Maeve whispered. "Do you see her, Maitland?"

"Aye, I see her. And those are definitely angel wings." They both stared at the woman, who looked oddly familiar to Maeve.

She waved her hands above her head and said, "Oh, I see. I thought there might be a problem. Just a moment." Then she disappeared and came back much smaller. "Is this better? Do ye recognize me now?"

"Callie! So you were not real, were you?" Maeve asked as she squeezed her husband's hand.

"I'm very real, but I don't live in yer world. I did what I needed to do for two very stubborn people. I had to get ye to follow me, and I knew ye'd never follow an adult. It had to be a child. I tried to push ye two together numerous times, but ye just were not listening. It's hard to set aside as much pain as both of yer hearts still carried. But it was time to move on. The universe wished for it."

"The universe?" Maitland had never heard such a word.

"It's what we angels call our world. All of Creation. We try to guide ye so ye can serve yer purpose here in life, but sometimes it's difficult to be heard through all the noise. Ye two had too much noise, so we decided to take some of it away."

"Away?" Maeve asked.

The child-like vision returned to her adult form. "Ye needed to get past losing your father and had to deal with the nightmares, Maeve. And Maitland, ye had to learn the truth, that Nesta's death was not yer fault. Ye would only believe it if ye heard it from her, which made it a wee bit difficult. As ye know, your angels don't normally appear to the living, but this was special. Please do not share our appearance with too many. Not that many would believe ye, but we prefer to keep it quiet. Others would be disappointed that it didn't happen for them. Do I make sense?"

"So ye are our guardian angel?"

"I am yer *guiding* angel. Yer guardian angel is someone different. She is the one who sent ye to Alex and Maddie, Maeve. Yer guardian angel, Maitland, protects ye on the battlefield. But I needed to rush this love match. There wasn't much time left."

Maitland looked at Maeve and asked, "Time? Is something going to happen?"

"Yer child needs to be born, and soon, Maeve will no longer be able to carry. I couldn't wait any longer."

Maeve's eyes widened. "We're going to have a bairn?" Her hand went right to her belly, rubbing it gently. Maitland's hand covered hers.

"In about eight months. I gave ye a little encouragement that night, and fortunately ye took the hint. Yer son has been waiting patiently, and he will live a long life. Ye'll only have one child, but he'll be a very special one. Trust in the universe, be kind, and enjoy yer love."

Her image began to fade, and she waved, blowing them a kiss. "And for Heaven's sake, pay attention next time!"

THE END

http://www.keiramontclair.com

D EAR READER,
    I wish you the happiest and healthiest holiday, whatever you celebrate!

Keira Montclair

NOVELS BY
KEIRA MONTCLAIR

HIGHLAND HUNTERS
THE SCOT'S CONFLICT
THE SCOT'S TRAITOR
THE SCOT'S PROTECTOR
THE SCOT'S VOW
THE SCOT'S DESTINY

HIGHLAND HEALERS
THE CURSE OF BLACK ISLE
THE WITCH OF BLACK ISLE
THE SCOURGE OF BLACK ISLE
THE GHOSTS OF BLACK ISLE
THE GIFT OF BLACK ISLE

THE CLAN GRANT SERIES
#1- RESCUED BY A HIGHLANDER-
Alex and Maddie
#2- HEALING A HIGHLANDER'S HEART-
Brenna and Quade
#3- LOVE LETTERS FROM LARGS-
Brodie and Celestina
#4-JOURNEY TO THE HIGHLANDS-
Robbie and Caralyn
#5-HIGHLAND SPARKS-
Logan and Gwyneth

#6-MY DESPERATE HIGHLANDER-
Micheil and Diana
#7-THE BRIGHTEST STAR IN THE
HIGHLANDS-
Jennie and Aedan
#8- HIGHLAND HARMONY-
Avelina and Drew
#9-YULETIDE ANGELS

THE HIGHLAND CLAN
LOKI-Book One
TORRIAN-Book Two
LILY-Book Three
JAKE-Book Four
ASHLYN-Book Five
MOLLY-Book Six
JAMIE AND GRACIE-Book Seven
SORCHA-Book Eight
KYLA-Book Nine
BETHIA-Book Ten
LOKI'S CHRISTMAS STORY-Book Eleven
ELIZABETH-Book Twelve

THE BAND OF COUSINS
HIGHLAND VENGEANCE
HIGHLAND ABDUCTION
HIGHLAND RETRIBUTION
HIGHLAND LIES
HIGHLAND FORTITUDE
HIGHLAND RESILIENCE
HIGHLAND DEVOTION
HIGHLAND BRAWN
HIGHLAND YULETIDE MAGIC

HIGHLAND SWORDS
THE SCOT'S BETRAYAL
THE SCOT'S SPY
THE SCOT'S PURSUIT
THE SCOT'S QUEST
THE SCOT'S DECEPTION
THE SCOT'S ANGEL

THE SOULMATE CHRONICLES TRILOGY
#1 TRUSTING A HIGHLANDER
#2 TRUSTING A SCOT
#3 TRUSTING A CHIEFTAIN

STAND-ALONE BOOKS
ESCAPE TO THE HIGHLANDS
THE BANISHED HIGHLANDER
REFORMING THE DUKE-REGENCY
WOLF AND THE WILD SCOTS
FALLING FOR THE CHIEFTAIN-3RD in a
collaborative trilogy
HIGHLAND SECRETS -3rd in a collaborative
trilogy

THE SUMMERHILL SERIES-CONTEMPORARY ROMANCE
#1-ONE SUMMERHILL DAY
#2-A FRESH START FOR TWO
#3-THREE REASONS TO LOVE

ABOUT THE AUTHOR

KEIRA MONTCLAIR IS the pen name of an author who lives in South Carolina with her husband. She loves to write fast-paced, emotional romance, especially with children as secondary characters.

When she's not writing, she loves to spend time with her grandchildren. She's worked as a high school math teacher, a registered nurse, and an office manager. She loves ballet, mathematics, puzzles, learning anything new, and creating new characters for her readers to fall in love with.

She writes historical romantic suspense. Her best-selling series is a family saga that follows two medieval Scottish clans through four generations and now numbers over forty books.

Contact her through her website:
keiramontclair.com

Made in the USA
Monee, IL
23 April 2024

57404902R00079